The Fantastical Adventures of Sleepy Steve: Reuniting the Stone

Jay,
Enjoy the book!

By Deronte' L. Smith

Deronte' Smith

© 2005

2005

An Infinity One Book in conjunction with Life Changing Books
Published by Infinity One Publishing
P.O. Box 725394 Atlanta, GA 31139

Cover art by Charlotte Riley-Webb
Edited by Elaine Smith
Layout by Brian Holscher

Library of Congress Control Number: 2005933662

ISBN 0977288803

Contents

Dedication

First and foremost I dedicate this book to the major influence in my life, our Heavenly Father; without YOU I could not have made it this far. Thank you for blessing me with a strong will to accomplish my dreams, a strong support system of people who believe in me and the many people who will find inspiration from this book.

I would like to thank Mrs. "Tina" Smith for giving me life, believing in me before I had any idea of what it was I wanted to do with my life and encouraging me to write what was in my heart at an early age. My strength, my courage, discipline and drive I derive from her as she was truly the strongest woman I will ever know – rest in peace momma.

For those who offered a kind word of encouragement, gave their time and energy to this project, offered a hand in just helping me stay afloat and helped to spread this project by word of mouth, I thank you for your continued support and prayers as this is only the beginning of the journey.

And last but certainly not least, I thank my family for supporting me down this long road. Shauna, thanks for the tough love to get me jumpstarted in the right direction. Dad, thanks for always telling me I can do whatever I set my mind to. Aunt Sarah, thanks for being that voice of reason when crucial decisions were being made. Grandma Dorothy and Lorena, your loving voices were always a comfort in the midst of the storm. Kim, I share a special relationship with you that is incomparable to any. Thank you for sticking by my side and for allowing me to come into your life. Mr. Imhotep Morgan, Mr. Nevins, Mr. Corell, and Dr. H.D. Flowers, though you are not family by blood you will always be a part of "my" family as your influence on my life has been tremendous.

Finally, thank you to all of my fans and anyone who purchases a copy of this book. Your support is appreciated and will never be forgotten.

Words from the Author

As long as I can remember, writing has been my favorite pastime wasting countless hours writing into the night until I fell asleep with my pen poking into my face. An elaborate storyteller, I have been called by people who know me best and know of my ability to whip up a fresh one from scratch. I recall a time when my writing was all I had to look forward to in the evening as television and video games were strictly forbidden in my house on school nights. So I learned the craft of creating visuals of characters in my mind and placing them in any given setting to see what they might do if they were real.

Before long I began to perfect my craft winning 4H contests for poetry and literary contests for dramatic writing essays. But none of this was enough to convince me that I could successfully pursue writing as a career until I got to college. It was there I soon found out that a pre-med major was not for me. Instead I was encouraged to study something that really interested me, something I enjoyed. I have always enjoyed writing, so I decided on English as a major – creative writing specially.

But, what you see before you was years in the making. After several years of gaining invaluable "real world" experience, I finally woke up one day to realize that my voice is needed and should be heard – as I feel yours is too. I talked with friends and family then decided to embark upon this journey that has culminated with the completion of this book. The funny thing is that the life experiences we have often play so heavily into what we will eventually become or do, but we just don't realize it at the time.

My point, when I walked across the stage of my high school graduation I will never forget a man by the name of Emmet "Buzz" Burnam introducing me to my classmates as "Dr. Deronte' Smith." As of today, I am about ten years out of college and I do not possess a MD or PHD yet, nor do I intend to pursue one. I wrote this book with the hope you, at whatever age you might be, will find inspiration in a young boy who learns to deal with his disability realizing there is a world of opportunities out there. Pursue your passion, chase your dreams and with some hard work you too can see your efforts come to fruition. Never let go of your dreams, for if you do you will wither and die – keep hope alive.

Chapter One

Super-Sleepy Stevie

The morning dew settles fresh atop the roof of the dusty gray two-story home as its occupants begin to stir within. BUZZZ! sounds the alarm clock by the nappy head of a kid who helms himself to be the prankster of pranksters, joker of the jokers, funniest of . . . well, you get the point.

"Stevie! Get up! It's time for school!" shouts the tender loving voice of his mother from downstairs. She paces to and fro, preparing her son's lunch, laying out sandwich meat, tomato, lettuce, bread and mayonnaise. In a sweeping scoop she dumps a huge spoon full of mayo onto his sandwich, then smears it evenly across the slice.

"Stevie, are you up yet?"

Inside Steve's bedroom, his chunky meat claw smacks the

1

alarm into a silent oblivion while the forces of nature act violently below, blowing ferocious smelly gas from the crack of his butt held together like two country hams by the band of his underwear. The dead silence allows his mom to acknowledge the fact that he is probably still in bed.

Deep in his sleep an old, wise ancient philosopher known as Confucius speaks to Steve, giving him guidance. Confucius says, "Steve, true knowledge comes from the wisdom contained within the pages of your school books, not just the hard lessons you will learn from life's experiences." In his dream, Steve stands, staring up at the white bearded man who appears older than Santa and larger than life. Steve rubs his eyes in disbelief, but the man is still there, floating in mid-air. Steve's attention is focused on the man's face, but he manages to reach deep into the pockets of his own pants. He pulls out a pack of chewing gum. Offering it up to the man he says, "Would you like some chewing gum, 'cause your breath is kinda tart?"

In a swift motion he lifts his cane into the air and whacks Steve on his forehead, replying, "Are you listening? This is not a joke. You are in the middle of your first years of life, but what have you truly accomplished? Have you discovered what you want to be?"

Steve stares blankly into the man's face. Confucius says, "Any ideas? Soon, Steve, you will be faced with decisions that will affect not only your life but the lives of people you love and those around you."

Steve looks teary-eyed as he internalizes what this might mean to his future.

From the distant room Steve hears the call of his mother "Stevie!" Poking her head just within the bedroom walls, she startles Steve from his dream as the old man's voice fades into the void.

"Remember, Steve, the answer lies in reuniting the stone!" Steve's mom walks into the room, whopping him with the Spiderman pillow that is lying at the foot of his bed. "Get up

2

before you're late! You don't want to start the school year out on the wrong foot, nor can I be late for work. The doctor wouldn't understand."

Steve grumbles, "OK, oK, ok," as he climbs from his bed and stops to wipe the sand from his eyes. With his clearing vision, he sees the outfit laid out for him at the foot of his bed. "Mom, I'm not wearing this! Mom did you hear me?"

"I heard you, but I don't think you have much of a choice," she replies. "That's what happens when you pass up a trip to the mall when you know I'm going school shopping. I just don't know what you were thinking," she says as she prepares her makeup in the bathroom mirror.

Steve stares intently at the clothing. "But all you bought were pink, light blue and light green."

She insists, "They're my favorite colors. And besides, I thought pastels were supposed to be in fashion this season." She smiles with a condescending grin.

"Sure, maybe if your name is Shirley!" he shouts, holding the shirt in front of the mirror.

His mother walks into the room. "All right already, what seems to be the problem? You used to look so cute in pink and baby blue."

"Mom, really! I'm not three years old anymore and I don't like tight, stretchy clothes," he scowls while pouting with his lips bunched up.

She grabs the fat dangling from his face squeezing his cheeks together. "Oh, pookie wookie, is my little Stevie growing up?"

Steve's eyes swell up with emotion. "Pookie wookie? Mom you have to stop calling me that! And my name's not Stevie anymore, either. They call me Steve now."

She shakes her head and steps toward the door, "And when did this come about?"

Steve strokes his brow to think. "Hmm, since about the fourth grade."

3

She chimes in sarcastically, "Wow, that's a really long time! Well, try this on for size, Steve. If you're not downstairs waiting by the door in exactly twenty-six minutes, you will find yourself on the bus."

A fading, dull yellow Twinkie with a patch of green mold on its side sits on Steve's nightstand beside the highly coveted Loews Super Summer movie pass. Steve plucks off the green spot, crams the Twinkie into his mouth, and squishes the cream through his teeth, standing in front of the mirror while he rolls his porky abdomen in waives. Picking up his black- fisted Afro pick, he shoves it into the roots of his hair, where it would seem no comb has gone before.

He tries to pull it out. "Ouch!" CLICK, POP, POP, POP! go the metal blades of the pick through his coarse hair. He makes a stern face at himself in the mirror and attempts a second stab at the thick abyss of tightly knotted curls that go beading down the top and sides of his head. The design of the rows is so intricate that it would be nearly impossible to fake his grade of hair for any staged production or event anyone could fathom doing. With more crispness than Snap, Crackle, and Pop! Steve reluctantly tries for a third and final time to make some sense out of the mop of hair with which he has been so graciously blessed.

"Mom, I give up! Can you fix my hair?"

She waltzes into the room, carrying her utensils carefully rolled in a freshly bleached white terry-cloth towel as if she were about to perform a surgical procedure. She places a pair of white rubber gloves over her hands. Snapping the band to her wrist in an almost mechanical motion, she squirts a watery mist into his hair, followed by a generous application of thick, heavy petroleum jelly that is known as Vaseline. She kneads the grease into his head as if she was making homemade biscuits, then slides the pick along side of his ears, strategically pulling the knots into straight strands. Within a couple of minutes Steve's hair is a greasy, one-inch mess of a mini-fro ball that was ready for the critics.

Dressed in his pastel pink, Steve resembles a bottle of Pepto-Bismol as he slides down the banister of the stairs. "Ta da, I'm ready!" he shouts out leaping from the banister rail, when suddenly CRASH!–the loving picture of Steve with his mother and father on a family vacation in the Smokey Mountains, framed in a stone picture frame, slams to the floor. Steve looks down at the frame, broken in three pieces. A quiet hurt settles on his chest as he realizes he has broken the only thing left linking his parents together as he so fondly remembers them.

Suddenly the voice of the old man echoes through the room. "Remember, Steve, your priority will be reuniting the stone."

Steve looks around the house, but all is quiet—too quiet. He heads to the kitchen and sees a note attached to his sack lunch. The note reads, "Sorry, buddy, but I had to go. Love ya, Mom."

He sighs, "This is what I'm talking about; Dad wouldn't have left me." He grabs the lunch and sadly approaches the broken picture and frame lying on the floor. He carefully picks the pieces from the floor and places them in his bag. Looking up, he sees his mom in the car through the window. In a mad panic he dashes through the door, with his bag in his hand.

Making his way to the sidewalk, he chases the car as it backs down the drive. "Hey wait up! Mom, wait up! I'm ready! I'm sorry, I promise I won't be late again!" Steve yells, trailing the car to the street.

She pulls up to the curb and rolls down the passenger side window. "What can I do for you Steve?"

"I need a ride to school. Come on, Ma! Stop playing."

She tries to hold back her laughter as she watches Steve squirm, trying to make up for his tardiness. "Sorry, son, at your very fragile and impressionable age I need to be firm in teaching you responsibility."

Steve frowns. "Says who?"

Looking into her review mirror, she smiles, noticing the

school bus pulling up from behind them. "Better Parenting For Dummies. Oh, look! There's the bus. I'm sure you don't want to miss them, too. Gotta go. Love you." A thin cloud from the car's exhaust spits into Steve's face as he watches his mother drive down the street.

Chapter Two

The Three

Rules of English

Steve walks reluctantly to the bus and climbs aboard. The bus driver is a creepy looking half-man, half-reptile type person with extremely scaly skin, heavy yellow eyebrows and a scruffy yellowish beard. The driver looks down over his dark mirror shades, extending his hand to Steve making his way to the top step. "Welcome aboard, laddie. And what would be your name?"

Steve puts his hands in his pockets quickly to prevent exchanging a handshake with him "Laddie? What's a laddie?"

The driver pauses to smile. "I am from Ireland, home of the leprechauns, and to the Irish, you see, young tots like yourself who are off to school each morning are what we call 'laddies.'"

"Oh," replies Steve. "Well, the name's Steve."

"Steve is it? There are just a few simple rules you must follow if you want to ride on Mr. English's—that's me—boat of fun."

Steve impolitely interrupts. "What boat? Isn't this is a bus?"

From two rows back, a pale, frail kid with a low fade for his hair style, wearing thick specs speaks up. "Humor him, he's a little. . ." the kid swirls his finger around in a circle by his head and whispers "crazy."

Steve nods in agreement.

"As I was saying, laddie, first you must be at or near your stop at precisely five minutes before your scheduled pickup. I have a lot of little people that I am responsible for getting to school on time, so if you're late you will be left. Got it?"

Steve sighs, "Got it."

"Second, when you reach the top of the steps you must be wearing a smile."

Steve interrupts. "What? You have to be kidding!"

Mr. English shuts the door. "Afraid not, laddie. On this bus we promote the absence of negativity, so by the time you reach school you will be in the correct mind frame to learn as much as possible."

Steve drags himself away from the overly cheery bus driver.

"Hey, you wanna sit beside me?" asks the kid with the thick glasses.

"Sure," Steve says as he sinks into the seat. "My name's Steve, that's short for Steven but my mom likes to call me Stevie."

"So which is it—Steve, Steven, or Stevie?" questions the little boy, with his forehead crunching into wrinkles.

"I prefer Steve. What's your name?"

"Charles Cornwallace Rodriguez the III," says the boy ever so proudly.

Steve responds, "You mean there was a first and a second with that name?"

The boy frowns. "No, my mom likes suffixes."

Steve adds, "Cornwallace sounds like Ben Wallace from the Detroit Pistons. Man, they're great!"

Charles quickly defends his heritage. "Wrong again; my great-great-great grandfather General Cornwallace was the brave leader from the American Revolution and his sons in the Confederate States of America."

"General Cornwallace? But you're black!" says Steve.

"Half Puerto Rican, half white," the boy explains.

"And the Confederates lost," Steve says.

Chuck adds, "but they lost for a cause." He sighs. "My mom says that's more vision than most people have today," exclaims the passionate kid.

Seeing that the boy is becoming upset, Steve changes the subject. "Man, that's a long name. Don't they call you anything else?"

Charles thinks for a second. "Actually, no."

"Sorry, that's too long, how about I just call you Chuck?" Steve asks as he opens the paper bag that contains his lunch.

"Chuck, I kinda like that. Yes, I think Chuck will work quite well. Chuck it is. I'm Chuck."

"You're so excited by the nickname. Don't you know that's what they call everybody whose name is Charles, just like they call everybody Dick whose name is Richard?"

Chuck laughs hard, all the way down inside his belly, "Dick? That's silly why would a grown man call himself that?" He continues, "What else do they say?"

Steve's eyes perk up as he sees his first opportunity to make a practical joke for the day. "Since you're asking, I hear that people named Charles are the first ones to die in their families, too."

A look of panic passes over Chuck's face. "What? Is that true?"

"Of course it's true. I said it didn't I? You're my newest friend. Do you really think I would lie to you?" With a devilish grin, Steve develops his plan, waving at a little girl a couple of

9

rows behind them.

"Hey, can I ask you a question, please?"

The girl is a tough one with kinky pigtails poking through her baseball cap, clad in faded jeans, an oversized tee and an old pair of sneakers. "What?" she asks, hovering above them while she chomps on her chewing gum.

"Haven't you heard that kids named Charles or Chuck are the first ones to die in their families?" Steve winks at her so as to not give away the prank.

"Uh, yeah, I think so, but that was a long time ago." She turns and walks back towards her seat.

Chuck wipes his brow. "This is all new to me. I didn't know any of this."

Steve tries to play off the joke by not showing any emotion. "Like she said, it was a long time ago, but I'm sure it's still true." Steve turns toward the girl walking down the aisle, "Hey, what is your name?" Noticing Mr. English's change of expression in the reflection of the front windshield, she hurries to her seat.

Steve stands, taking a couple of steps towards her. "Hey, I said what is your name?"

Suddenly, the bus comes to a complete halt and every kid on the bus comes to absolute straight attention. Chuck taps Steve on his shoulder. "Um, Steve you might want to sit down."

Steve glances down at him. "For what? And why is the bus stopping?"

The usual warming rays of the morning sun change tempo, casting the huge dark shadow of Mr. English engulfing the bus's interior, bringing terror to the hearts of the boys and girls within. With enormously large steps, Mr. English walks up behind the unsuspecting Steve. With a loud thunderous *clap!* above Steve's head, he quickly brings to Steve's attention that his behavior is unwelcome.

"Mr. Steve, do you see this sign that I so politely pointed out to you this morning?"

10

Steve's eyes are as big as wet circular imprints of coke cans on loose- leaf paper. He shakes his head in agreement, fighting to hold back his fear.

Mr. English continues. "Item number three on this nicely laminated piece of paper says in big **BOLD** print, 'Thou shalt not walk while the bus is in motion.'"

He pauses to look up at the rest of the wide-eyed audience. "Does everyone here understand that very plain and simple rule?"

"Yes," they reply.

"I know this is your first day on my fun boat, but you will follow the rules or you will not continue to ride with us. As I said, there are no exceptions to the rules. OK?"

Steve shakes his head.

"Now, if there are no more interruptions, let's get back to having fun," says Mr. English, re-positioning himself behind the steering wheel.

The bus pulls off. Steve folds his arms pouting from the embarrassment. "Boat of fun! This is more like the bus of nightmares."

Chuck peeks into Steve's sack, examining what he is having for lunch. "Don't take it personal, he just wants everyone to follow the rules."

Steve huffs. "My dad used to say rules are meant to be broken."

"So does mine, but then my mom says you have to know the rules in order to know which ones to break." Chuck smiles. "What do you mean *used to*? You make it sound like your dad is dead."

Steve's head tilts toward the ground and his mood suddenly changes. "He's not dead, but my parents split up last year. I don't know what happened; all I know is that my mom took a job here and we moved. It's been a tough year, and now I have to deal with school."

Chuck looks on at Steve in disbelief. "Man, that's crazy!

You're parents split up and now you're dad's not around?"

Steve nods his head. "I haven't seen him in over a year. I don't know where he is, and mom tells me not to ask."

Chuck feels the tension from the conversation and tries to lighten the moment by looking through Steve's bag. "Your mom must not be much of a cook."

Steve pauses. "Why do you say that?"

Chuck sighs. "'Cause no one eats cold cuts on the first day of school. That's like taking your own popcorn to the movies; you just don't do it."

The boys burst into laughter, although the rest of the bus is unaware of their fun.

"And you have no snacks. Here, take some of mine." Chuck pulls a couple of snacks from his pockets, then asks, "Do you realize how much a cookie at school costs these days?"

Steve looks down at his bag with disappointment. "No, how much are they?"

Snooping in on their conversation, the little girl comes up from behind, "One dollar fifty, and they ain't very big. Hey, are you new or something? 'Cause I didn't see you around last year."

"Yes," Steve replies,

"You look kinda big for a sixth grader," the girl states calmly.

"This is my second time in the sixth grade. I didn't make the cut last year," says Steve, looking unsatisfied with his sandwich and causally blowing off his failure of the previous school year as if he didn't make the football team.

"You mean you failed?" Chuck asks in awe.

"No, I mean I got held back—for medical reasons. I have problems staying awake sometimes, which makes it kind of hard to pass the tests, especially Mrs. Wrigley's from Fort Knox."

The girl pulls the chewing gum from her mouth, glancing forward to make sure Mr. English does not catch her as she

12

tucks the sticky soft gum wad under the seat. She adds, "I hear she's pretty mean. My sister had her. She's a real genius, and she barely passed."

The boys reply together, "Wow!"

Steve gains more interest in what the girl has to say. "You're from Fort Knox?"

"No, we just lived there for a while. My parents are military, so we bounce all over."

"I hear that's a hard way to live; my dad is a reservist," says Steve.

Chuck replies, "What's Fort Knox?"

Steve answers, "It's only the richest place in the world! It's where all the gold is kept."

The girl piggybacks his comment. "It's a federal reserve for gold. It used to be one of the largest, but I think it has gotten too old for them to use it now. It's more of a tourist spot these days."

Chuck's eyebrows lift with curiosity, "Gold? You mean they have gold there!"

The girl speaks up, "Used to. Like I said, I don't think they keep much there anymore."

Struggling to get his words out, Chuck says, "Man, moving around all the time you must be one tough cookie."

Steve looks at the girl's rough appearance. "Speaking of tough cookies, what is your name?"

She laughs. "Who's tough? Not little ol' me?" She punches Chuck in his arm.

Chuck responds, "Ouch! That hurt!"

She pulls back, her fist aimed at Steve. "What about you, are you a cry baby too?"

Steve curls his arm up to his chin, making his best muscle. "Go ahead, take your best shot."

The girl winds up her fist and delivers a hard blow to Steve's chest, rocking his chest plate. Steve falls to the cushion of the seat, gasping for air while the girl moves away from the seat, shaking her head in disgust.

Chuck, in an effort to stop her, says, "You nearly killed him. Where are you going?"

The bus pulls up beside a sign reading "East Cobb Sixth Grade Academy." Throwing her book bag over her shoulders, the girl replies to Chuck, "To school. You guys are wimps." She exits the bus, leaving Steve still trying to recover from her gut punch.

Chuck picks his bag from the floor and stands to exit. "Are you all right, dude? You look a little pale."

Steve takes a deep breath to regain his breath. Exhaling, he says, "Man, she's got a serious punch."

Chapter Three

New Beginnings

Steve stands and exits the bus with his newly found friend, Chuck, along with the rest of the children. The schoolyard is flooded with kids of all shapes and sizes—running, jumping, and tumbling in every direction just before the bell rings. Steve and Chuck drag themselves to the set of double doors, where the beginning of their sixth grade experience awaits. Chuck steps within the doors confidently, leaving Steve behind with a look of suspicion on his face. Chuck tugs at his shirt, encouraging him to come in, while the other kids dart around them, standing in the middle of the entrance.

Chuck says, "Steve, come in man! You can't just stand in the doorway all day."

Steve replies, "I don't know about this. Maybe I should just go back to my old school."

Chuck glances up at the clock. "You can't. You moved, remember? Stop playing before you make us late for class."

Steve steps through the doorway, pausing to relax against the inner hallway wall, pulling a snack from a secret compartment within his book bag while Chuck stands beside him, waiting impatiently. He wolfs down the snack within a matter of seconds, crumples up the wrapper, tossing it inside his bag as he reaches for another. Opening the candy bar, Steve stuffs it in between his lips, nibbling on the chocolate layer.

Chuck cries, "What in the world are you doing?"

Steve crams another bite of the snack into his mouth. "I'm nervous. I eat when I'm nervous."

Chuck sighs. "I can see that."

Steve reacts, "What is that supposed to mean?"

"Nothing more than that you're a plump kid. You should really watch what you eat; you could be putting yourself at risk for diabetes or heart problems," says Chuck with concern.

Steve blows him off. "That's hogwash, my mom says I'm just a little healthy, that's all."

Chuck laughs "That means *fat*."

Within minutes the fun ceases and the school day begins at the chime of a loud metal bell. Steve and Chuck walk up to the wall where the homeroom for each student is posted. Chuck scrolls down the long list and quickly finds his name. "Mr. Rowe. Whose class do you have?"

Steve casually steps up to the list, in no apparent hurry at the sound of the bell. He shoves the last of his snacks down his throat, finally seeing his name. "Mr. Rowe too. Cool, we've got first period together." The boys grab their bags and head down the hallway.

The hallway is a dull, moldy green with Swiss cheese colored tile, stretching like a long, winding tree with branches reaching in every direction. It leads to other hallways and corridors that have more hallways and corridors, that have rooms upon rooms down each of the corridors. It is an immense maze of puke-green confusion with no end in sight, spanning three times the length of the football field.

"This way," says Steve, who strolls off toward the hallway to the left.

Chuck follows. "Are you sure? This doesn't feel right."

Walking down the long hall, the traffic whirls past them, thinning down to an almost calming stillness.

"Dude, this is not cool," Chuck says, tapping Steve on his back.

Steve continues in the same direction until they come to room A-19. Steve glances up, "I think that's it." They continue down the hall a short distance more. Just as they reach their homeroom, the eerie squeak of a rusty door comes from the shadows of the stairwell.

Chuck looks at Steve. "What's that?"

Steve peeks around the corner. "I don't know. Whatever it is, I'm not sticking around to find out."

Steve and Chuck take a step towards the door when the sunny interior of the hallway suddenly grows dark.

Steve notices that the light is blocked by the big head of the tough pig- tailed girl from the bus. She is heading in their direction. Surely fate could not be playing such a cruel joke on them, but indeed it was. As they approach the classroom door, she runs up, huffing and puffing and grabs the door away from the two boys. She holds the door open, letting them walk in first.

"Wimps before girls," she taunts, smacking Chuck on his butt.

Chuck hurries through the door into the classroom. She pulls the elastic band on Steve's briefs, snapping them back into place as she laughs hysterically.

Startled, Steve nearly jumps out of his skin. "Watch out, you big lug! I'm not afraid of you. You sucker-punched me on the bus, but that won't happen again." She dances in circles around

17

the boys.

They stand, mystified by her arrogance. "You're a big teddy bear. My puppy pit bull is scarier than you."

She walks off, and the boys turn to take their seats near the back of the room. A middle-aged man stands at the front of the classroom, clearing his throat for the room to quiet down.

Chapter Four

Fun Work

With the loudness of the kids coming from every corner of the classroom, the teacher makes a plan to get their attention. Slowly, he retakes his seat and skillfully pulls a thick book from his drawer, placing it firmly on his desk. Suddenly he slams the book together, grabbing the immediate attention of the class. The class comes to a hushing silence, threatened by the unexpected actions of the teacher, who is desperate to gain their attention and respect.

Standing from his chair, he moves to the center of the room and addresses the class. "Now that I have your attention, good morning, class. I would like to welcome you on your first day of school. I am Mr. Rowe. Many of you may know me from Clayton Elementary, as I transferred this year. For those of you who don't, let me assure you that this will be a year of fun-filled learning exercises. They have been designed by the top scholastic minds in the country to maximize the information you will be expected to retain in order to meet your objectives for the aptitude tests administered at the end of the school year."

He looks around at the class. Crickets chirp in the dead silence as everyone looks at him with glazed-over eyes. He realizes he needs to rephrase his introduction to the class. "Ok, in layman's terms, in this class this year you will not have any homework. Our goal will be to focus on having fun, while experimenting with learning." The class goes wild with whistles and cheers, while Chuck seems to be the only student unimpressed by the newly implemented style of teaching from Mr. Rowe.

Steve cheers from the back of the room, "*Funwork!*" The kids cheer him on even louder.

"Yeah, Funwork!"

Steve looks at Chuck with a puzzled expression. "What's the matter? He said no homework. Doesn't that sound great?"

Chuck pulls a magazine from his book bag. "The problem is that my mind needs to absorb as much as possible before the SAT exams by my sophomore year. I intend to gain my acceptance into Stanford by my 17th birthday, but I can't do it if school's going to be all about having fun!"

Steve reacts. "What? That's the dumbest thing I have ever heard. You serious?"

Chuck stands from his seat, interrupting the celebration. "Excuse me, Mr. Rowe. I don't mean to sound pessimistic, but just how is this new system of learning going to increase our readiness for collegiate testing that's only a couple of years down the road?"

Mr. Rowe stands, looking shocked, unprepared to answer the question of the brainy child who has little common sense.

A little girl, dressed in a pink lacy top with ruffles and a skirt that settles just above her knees, stands, coming to Mr.

Rowe's aid. "Let me handle this. Look little boy, not everyone requires tons of homework just to learn a bunch of crap that we probably already know anyway. Personally, I welcome the break of constantly having to rush through four or five assignments every night, missing out on my favorite T.V. shows."

The kids back her up. "Yeah, me too."

By now Mr. Rowe has regained his composure. "The teaching style is called cooperative learning, and yes, she makes a point. And your name, young lady?"

She stands, smiling at the class as if the classroom is a theatrical stage, and the spotlight momentarily shines on the brilliance of her brief performance. Consumed with admiration, the class is her audience, awaiting her next move. She skirts to center stage, taking a bow before Mr. Rowe. "I am the ever-talented Ms. Ella Mae Vanwagoneer at your service, but you may call me Ms. Elle, sir."

Mr. Rowe is speechless at her bold actions and soaring confidence as she continues. "I sing, I dance, but mostly importantly, I embrace the artistic qualities of life."

Mr. Rowe looks pleasantly surprised "Well, I must say your resumé sounds impressive. It looks like we are definitely in for some entertainment this year." Just as he finishes his sentence, a short kid with big brown eyes, mixed black and blonde choppy hair, high water pants and a pair of dusty penny loafers steps through the door.

Mr. Rowe invites the boy in. "Hello there! Come in and join us."

The boy takes the nearest open seat, which is directly behind Chuck.

Mr. Rowe picks up his list of homeroom roll while the students wait patiently. "Ah, you must be Sammy Patel." Mr. Rowe stands, showing a bright awkward smile, as the boy shakes his head shyly. "I'm sorry I forget, are you from Northern India or the south?"

The boy's eyebrows lift to see that he has some knowledge

21

of his country. "Southern India."

"Ah, Southern India. That's an interesting place. I spent some time there during my tour through Asia just after the war. I was in the artillery division of the Marines."

Momentarily, Mr. Rowe has just found a possible means of reaching the boys of his class who give each other high-fives upon learning that Mr. Rowe is an ex-Marine.

One of the boys speaks out. "Cool, you were a Marine. Did you ever kill anybody?"

Another boy screams out from the corner, "Yeah, I'll beat you killed a bunch of people!"

"Boys, that's a misperception, the Marines are not about all about killing people. Sure we had combat, but it was mostly for training unless you got into a predicament that you really didn't want to be caught in," replies Mr. Rowe.

The boy from the corner responds. "Then what good is it carrying a gun?"

Mr. Rowe quickly addresses the response. "It's about having the discipline not to use it and knowing the consequences of when you do."

The boy answers back, "My brother has a gun; he says it's for protection. He says it's rough out there in the streets."

Mr. Rowe pauses for a second, thinking about how to answer the confused kid. He asks the boy, "How old is your brother?"

He replies, "Sixteen."

Mr. Rowe responds, "Young man, I would dare say your brother doesn't realize he could be facing jail time if he was caught with that gun, considering that he is underage. And what happens if he gets into a situation where he feels he actually has to use it?"

Though Mr. Rowe addresses one boy in the back of the classroom, the rest of the class listens carefully at the mention of jail time. He paces the aisle, "The fact of the matter is, children, life is about choices. You can chose to carry a gun, perhaps to make you feel more secure with your environment or your 'hood,' but the harsh truth is that if you hurt or kill someone, you will do jail time. Anyway there's no joy in killing people." Mr. Rowe's face turns pale white, as if he has just seen a ghost, "Take my advice; avoid it at all costs. On that note. . ."

He makes a sharp turn toward the board. "Today is the first day of the rest of your lives. You will become enlightened with self-study that will affect the choices you will make in the consequent days ahead." He looks around at the class, and again their eyes are glazed over.

Finally, out of frustration, the little girl with the pigtails asks, "Excuse me, Mr. Rowe, why do you talk like that? We're just in the 6th grade. You give some good advice, but it's hard to understand you at times."

His nervous habit kicks in, swallowing hard enough to see the lump slide down the throat of his skinny neck like a tangerine. "Um, OK, I'm sorry. I will try to do much better explaining myself."

Standing from her seat, she walks toward the front of the room. "Have you ever heard of the rule of K.I.S.S?"

"No, I haven't," he adds, pushing his glasses up on his nose. "Why don't you share its meaning with the class."

The girl walks to the board, picks up a pick of chalk, and begins to write big bold letters, in a vertical line, down the blackboard. "K.I.S.S. stands for **K**eep. . .**I**t. . .**S**imple. . . **S**tupid!"

The kids burst into laughter as Mr. Rowe turns four different shades of red. "Young lady, one more outburst like that from you and you can expect to find yourself in detention for a week. Take your seat, please. Class, class, that will be enough!" He tries to regain control of his room. Steve grabs his stomach in laughter, while Chuck wipes away the tears from his eyes. They share a high-five with the girl, who keeps a straight face throughout the whole ordeal.

Steve nudges her arm, "That was a good one! You're OK with me."

Mr. Rowe dances around the room, trying to get everyone back into place after the disruption.

Suddenly the girl stands from her seat taking a bow. The kids roar in cheers, and she gently waves them into silence. "I'm sorry, Mr. Rowe. I didn't mean anything by it, but we're just kids. Maybe you should try to think back to when you were our age." She delicately chooses her words and then takes her seat.

"And your name young lady?" he asks.

"Ieka Fuller, sir," she says in a sincere tone.

"Ms. Fuller, you do understand that your interruption has cost us precious class time?" he notes.

She nods, agreeing, when all of a sudden a loud *crash* sounds from behind her seat.

On the floor, an antique violin lies, along with several books and sheets of paper that have scattered across the stained tile of the classroom floor. The violin, books and papers belong to Sammy, who drops quickly to his knees to collect his belongings.

Steve reaches to help the Indian kid, when he realizes the sheets are covered. Holding one of the sheets in the air, he loudly announces to the class, "Hey these sheets are covered in musical notes!"

The Indian kid snatches the piece of paper from Steve's hands, crams the papers into his satchel and tenderly holds the violin in his lap.

Mr. Rowe walks to up to the kid. "Sammy, do you write music?"

He nods his head, adding solemnly, "I play, too."

The kids turn their attention to the center of the room, as Mr. Rowe continues to question the boy about his talents.

Mr. Rowe strokes the scraggly cat whiskers he calls his mustache. "You obviously play the violin."

"And the bassinet, the clarinet, the obo, and the piano," says Sammy, with a smile on his face.

"Wow!" the kids respond, their mouths wide open.

"Is that possible?" Steve asks Chuck.

Chuck nods his head in amazement. "Certainly anything's possible, but that would make him some sort of prodigy."

Chapter Five

Too Much Excitement to Stay Awake

Mr. Rowe pats Sammy on his back. "Class, I believe with the diversity of talents we have in our class this year, we will have a very entertaining school year."

Sammy tucks his violin back into his bag, and Mr. Rowe returns to the front of the room.

Steve extends his hand to Sammy. "My name's Steve. This is Chuck."

Sammy shakes his hand. "I'm Sammy."

Steve looks down at the violin, concealed in the bag. "Can you really play that thing?"

Sammy nods. "I've been playing since I was three."

Chuck blurts out with excitement, "See? I told you he was a child prodigy! But wait, that wouldn't make sense. Why would you be in class with us?"

Sammy smiles, "I have to pass up chance to go to 8th grade because my father wants me to have–how do you say, um. . .American education. So sorry, my English is very poor."

Chuck drops back into his seat. "Unbelievable!"

Steve sees a piece of paper with a gold seal in its top corner, looking as if it might be an important document, sticking out of Sammy's notebook. Out of brash curiosity, Steve sneaks the paper from the notebook on the sly while Sammy is talking with Chuck. Steve studies the paper and discovers Sammy comes from a very important cast of people in his homeland. Steve nudges Chuck's arm, handing him the paper. "Look at this. I think Patel is royalty or something!"

Chuck quickly surveys the paper. "No, this says you have diplomatic immunity. Is that true, Sammy?"

Sammy sits silently, unsure of how to answer the question without putting off his overly curious classmates. Finally, he decides that maybe the best answer is the truth. "Yes, my dad is a diplomat in Spain. He is advisor to the national council."

Chuck is stumped, but it is clear from Sammy's disposition that he does not want to expose this to the rest of the class and get treated differently.

Steve clearly sees Chuck's reaction and Sammy's concern for the importance on the document, but his confusion lies in the fact that he simply doesn't know what Chuck is talking about.

Steve innocently asks, "Ok, fill me in, Brains. What the heck is diplomatic immunity?"

Sammy speaks up. "I get special privileges because of my father's position."

Chuck adds, "Yeah, like it's almost impossible for him to get into trouble because he is protected by the government—our government." Sammy's lowers his head into his lap. Chuck pats him on the back. "Don't worry, your secret's safe with us."

Steve adds, "Yeah, we won't tell anyone. I promise."

The students climb back into their seats when they hear the ring of the bell for the beginning of first period. Mr. Rowe steps to the front of the class, with a poster board dissected into five rows. "Class, for the rest of the period I am going to let you work on your in-class assignment that is due Monday. Many of you might find the assignment to be a piece of cake, and some may even think it's a joke, but remember, your assignments will count toward a large portion of your grade by the middle of the semester. I encourage you to take your work seriously."

Steve mumbles, "Yeah, yeah, so what is the assignment?"

Mr. Rowe catches Steve mumbling. "I'm sorry, young man. Did you say something?"

Steve grabs his mouth, "Nope, uh, what I said was I cannot wait to get the assignment."

Chuck smacks his head. "When will he ever learn?"

Mr. Rowe drags out the introduction of the assignment for another fifteen minutes, talking about what he expects out of each of his pupils. The assignment is broken down into five teams of five, for a total of twenty-five classmates. Each team is appointed a lead boy or girl, who is elected by their fellow teammates. The team leader will then work with his or her group to construct a series of questions that will help the other members of the team learn about their teammates.

The collected information is to be put into a summary for a group presentation to the class on Monday. The group with the most informative and creative way to share the information will win points toward a class prize for the end of the year. As Mr. Rowe divides the class into teams, the kids scramble to organize their desks into circles to choose their team leaders and get the assignment underway. Side by side 'til the end, Steve and Chuck are stuck together like Juicy Fruit to the bottom of a shoe as they sit respectively in their group.

Pigtails pulls her chair up beside Chuck, making him slightly nervous as he recalls the power of her punch from the bus. Music boy slides into the semi-circle just to the left of

Steve, as Ms. Elle—the queen diva herself—brings the circle to a close. She says, "Given that I am the person here with the most noted talents, and because I have appeared on Nickelodeon twice. And of course I was the Gerber baby; I think it is only right that I lead this group to its days of fame and popularity."

Steve speaks up. "It's true you might be the most animated of the group, but you're definitely not the most talented. I'll bet my boy Patel here could run circles around you any day of the week."

They all smack high-fives as the Indian boy chimes in correcting him. "Thank you, sir, but my name is Sammy. Like yours is Ste-vie."

He replies, "Steve—just call me Steve."

Ieka has had enough of the bickering. "Look, I know who will lead."

The group sits, quietly awaiting her suggestion. "Me," she says, without cracking a smile.

Steve bounces up from his seat. "What?"

She stares him down. "Any problems with that?"

He momentarily cowers in his seat. "Not here."

Ieka grabs Steve's sack lunch and sets it in the steel bookrack under her seat. "The first item of business is what I'm having for lunch."

Steve grabs his lunch away from her. "OK, enough is enough! I betcha it won't be my sandwich—not today!"

Chuck quickly speaks up to distract the female bully. "Children, children! Must we argue? We have some very important work here that needs to be handled. Let us keep our focus on the matter at hand, which is getting this assignment completed."

She calmly reclaims her seat, as Chuck takes charge of the group. He asks, "Does anyone have any good suggestions for questions we can ask each other?"

Ms. Elle quickly throws her hand forward, pointing at Ieka.

"I have one: is she a boy or a girl?"

The kids laugh, while Ieka wets her fingertips with saliva, smoothing down her sideburns to her face and gazing at her reflection in the surface of her desk. Ieka wipes the excess spit from her hands onto her pants.

Ms. Elle reacts. "Yuck! That's just gross."

Chuck attempts to get the group back on track. "I have a suggestion. I say let's start with the obvious. No offense, Sammy, but we'll start with you, since you are the most interesting."

Pulling out his notebook Steve hands it to Ms. Elle, who is fixing her face in her pocket mirror.

"Here," Steve says, handing off the notebook to her.

She takes the notebook, asking, "What's this for?"

"To take notes," he says, brushing her off.

Being the diva that she is, Ms. Elle can't believe Steve has the nerve to seriously suggest that she take notes for the group. She acts displeased. "I'm sorry, but I am not a secretary. This is the age of feminism, equal rights, and women's equality. I will not tolerate this cruelty and down right chauvinism."

Steve shakes his head, disagreeing. "No, take a piece of paper and pass it around so that we can take notes."

She replaces the pouting with a smile. "Oh, that's more like it."

Steve pushes his chair closer, toward the center of the group, preparing to make a big announcement. He is so excited he can hardly contain himself. "Guys, I have a great idea!" With their attention hanging on a thread, the group holds their breath, waiting to see what could be the announcement of the century! Steve pauses, just as he is about to release from his lips the words that were holding the group captive. Their faces show the stress they feel for what seems like an eternity.

"I can't take it anymore, Steve! What is it?" screams out Chuck.

Steve yawns, and suddenly his head drops into the seam of

31

the book open atop his desk.

Chuck cannot believe Steve's timing in falling asleep. How could he be so selfish as to deprive them of the profound idea he was about to share with him and his fellow classmates?

Chuck yells, "That's not fair! Wake up!" The kids are puzzled at Steve falling asleep so suddenly.

Sammy asks, "What's wrong with him? Is he dead?"

Chuck shows his irritation. "No, he's asleep."

From the front of the room, Mr. Rowe sits in an upright position in perfect posture at his desk. His eyes scan the computer screen of the laptop he is so intently studying. With the slight adjustment of his neck, he notices Steve lying face down in his book.

Standing up from his desk, he discretely circles the room, peeking over the students' shoulders to insure that they are working on the assignment, while his real motive is to find out what is going on with Steve.

Sliding up from the rear, he taps Steve on his shoulder, without the group realizing he is standing above them. Steve does not react to Mr. Rowe's attempt to awaken him.

Ms. Elle happens to glance up, seeing the tall, awkward man lingering above them. She wails out a scream so loud that it could pierce the eardrums of a dead man.

The teacher reacts in shock. "Elle, I'm sorry. I didn't mean to startle you kids."

She regains her composure. "It's OK."

He continues, "I am just trying to find out what is going on here with Steve."

Through all of the shoulder tapping, screaming and talking, nothing has awakened Steve from his sound sleep.

Chuck waves the teacher into the circle as if he was about to tell him the cure for cancer or the formula for the fountain of youth. The professor bends, with his head resting just above Chuck's ear. "He has a sleeping disorder; sometimes he just goes to sleep."

Remembering that he read the notes on Steve's condition, Mr. Rowe stands, with new understanding for the situation. "Oh, he is the sleeping boy. Don't worry, boys and girls. I know just the trick to bring him around." He walks back to his desk, then quickly returns.

Mr. Rowe places a bag of chips in front of Steve's face, and with a quick tug he opens the seal, allowing the aroma to waffle before Steve's nose, sending him into a hunger fit. Steve's head springs up from the desk, and with red eyes and all, he makes a fast move at the bag of chips in Mr. Rowe's hands. Mr. Rowe allows Steve a couple of chips before taking the bag away and returning to the front of the class.

Chuck shakes his head in disbelief, looking at Steve, who has aptly recovered from one of his sleeping spells at the scent of food. Chuck mumbles to himself, "The man is a genius!"

Ieka, having been thoroughly entertained by all of the excitement, is now fully interested in what is going on with the group. She looks Steve squarely in his eyes, saying, "What the heck is going on, Steve? Why do you fall asleep all of a sudden and wake up when food comes around?"

Steve shrugs her off. "I don't know; I just get sleepy sometimes."

Chuck adds in, "It's a very rare disorder known as narcolepsy, where its victims find themselves asleep without any notice at all."

Steve looks agitated. "Thanks Chuck."

Chuck smiles. "Don't mention it."

Ieka laughs, "Maybe we should call you Sleepy Steve."

The group reacts in favor of the suggestion, cheering her on. "Yeah. That sounds good."

Steve quickly adds, "I don't like that."

Ieka speaks up, "So? Nicknames aren't for you to like, or else what would be the point?"

Sammy says the nickname, pronouncing it with his thick Indian accent. "Slee-py Ste-ve."

They all break out in laughter, and the tone is set for the rest of the day, with Steve accepting his new nickname. Steve finds comfort in his new group of friends coming to understand his sleeping disorder.

Chapter Six

Valley of Death

Sitting in front of the class, relaxed and at ease, Mr. Rowe reads a novel by one his favorite authors. He notices the temperature throughout the morning has gradually gotten colder, and now his breath drifts in front of his face. He peeks over the rim of his book to see the glowing red noses of some of the students, lit up like Christmas lights, but it's only September. They are grouped together, tightly trying to keep the heat between themselves. The situation has gotten out of control. Looking down at his watch, Mr. Rowe figures out how much time is left in the period.

He addresses the class. "Excuse me, class. I must say I am proud of you guys for working together so well, but I need to ask you, am I the only one in here that is experiencing some climate discomfort?"

The class does not understand the question. He makes another attempt, asking, "Is anyone else in here is cold?"

They reply, "Yes, yes."

From the corner, the little boy answers "Yes, I've been cold all morning."

Chuck adds in, "It is unseasonably chilly today, for some strange reason."

Mr. Rowe looks at his roll call list, raising his head and looking toward the middle of the room. "Steve, could you please go down the hall to the janitor's closet and let him know I would like to speak with him briefly?"

Steve shutters with the thought of having to approach the creepy, dark closet under the stairwell all by his lonesome. Steve raises his hand immediately. "Mr. Rowe, I'm not exactly sure where that is. Can I take someone with me?"

He dismisses the question. "Don't be silly; it's just around the corner."

Steve realizes he needs to come on stronger with his concern, as Mr. Rowe is not going to be easily convinced. Interrupting the concentration on his book, Steve makes a ploy to readdress, Mr. Rowe who by now is comfortably poised at his desk. "Mr. Rowe, I'm sorry, but I need Chuck to go with me."

Chuck jumps in his seat. "Me?"

Steve kicks his shoe. "You see, sir, it's kind of dark and creepy where the janitor's closet is."

Mr. Rowe does not pay Steve too much attention. "Fine, you boys go, but return quickly so we get some heat in here before the end of the period."

Steve smiles with satisfaction, "Thank you." He steps toward the door, with Chuck clamping down to his chair. Steve walks back to Chuck's desk, urging him to get up. "Come on, we've got a job to do."

"No, not me. You volunteered for that, not me," says Chuck, who avoids eye contact with Steve.

Steve says, agitated, "Chuck, stop being such a wuss! Nothing's going to happen, I promise."

Chuck looks unconvinced. "You promise? You're always promising! How can you promise that? You're just as new here as I am."

Finally, out of frustration, Steve grabs Chuck's arm, prying him from his desk. Chuck gives in, "Look, I'm gonna do this for you, but we had better not get into any trouble."

Mr. Rowe glances up from his desk to see the boys still in the back of the room, "Boys, what seems to be the matter?"

Steve replies, "Oh nothing, sir. Chuck had to lace up his shoes." He gives Chuck a mean stare, whispering under his breath, "Let's go."

The boys step from the classroom, beginning their voyage down the hall to the dreaded janitor's closet where darkness awaits them. As they walk, they begin pushing and shoving each other playfully, tripping into the bulletin board that lines the hallway. The task is dull and boring, but the boys manage to find a way to make it interesting along the way.

A woman with extremely white freckly skin, big red bushy hair, red eyebrows and pink lips walks down the hallway, coming toward the boys. She has a badge clipped to her waist and walks, slouching, with very bad posture. She comes to a dead stop just as the boys are about to walk past, lowering a stiff arm like a toll bridge gate.

"Excuse me. Where are you boys going?"

Steve replies, "Our teacher, Mr. Rowe, sent us to the janitor's closet."

She frowns. "And where are your hall passes?"

A defeated look comes across Steve face, tucking his head into his chest. "Sorry, we don't have one."

The lady proudly pulls her badge from her waist, pushing it into Steve's face. "Tell me something, what does that say?"

Steve stumbles over his words. "It says 'Hall Monitor.'" He takes a deep breath, ready for her to lash out at them, when all of a sudden Chuck pulls the long plastic pass from his back pocket.

"Speak for yourself, Chubby." He laughs, robbing the Hall Monitor of her chance at giving them a piece of her mind.

Steve looks up in shock. "What? Where did you get that?"

The Hall Monitor rolls her eyes and walks away, extremely dissatisfied, in the other direction.

Chuck points for Steve to continue down the hall. "It was hanging by the door, so I thought I should grab it."

Steve gives Chuck some dap. "Good thinking."

From far in the distance, the loud creaking of the door grabs the boys' ears. Approaching the closet at a snail's pace, it seems the slower they walk, the bigger their steps become, inching them much closer to the janitor's room. Within only a stone's throw from the door, Steve and Chuck realize they are much closer to the uncertainty that awaits them behind the door than they really want to be. The sunlight shifts at the end of the hall, causing a shadow to partially cover Chuck's face when . . . *boom!*. . . the heavy metal door slams shut only ten feet away from where they stand. The sweat is dripping from their brow. Neither Steve nor Chuck could determine if they saw someone entering or leaving the room.

"Yea, though I walk through the valley of the shadow of death, I shall fear no evil. . ." Steve quotes the scripture, while squeezing the back of Chuck's arm. "Thy rod and thy staff shall comfort me. . ." Steve squints his eyes together, continuing to recite the Bible verse.

Chuck looks at Steve in amusement. "What are you doing?"

Steve sighs. "I'm praying. What does it look like?"

"OK then, what rod and what staff are you talking about?"

Steve replies, "You should really go to church sometimes."

Chuck looks Steve deeply in his eyes. "Are you scared?"

Steve retaliates. "No! I felt like praying, that's all. What's wrong with that?"

Chuck shrugs his shoulders. "Nothing. It's just that usually when most people pray in situations like this, they are scared."

Steve replies with confidence. "I said I am not scared, and if you're not scared, then let's go." Steve sucks in his gut and pushes out his chest, taking a bold step forward.

With only the worst in mind, they approach the great door, walking softly on their tiptoes as if they are walking on eggshells, trying not to make a sound. A warm breeze blows from the crack of the great door, carrying the sweet scent of two-day-old pastrami.

Steve tilts his head to the sky, with his nostrils flaring open to catch a whiff of the scent. "Do you smell that? It's pastrami on rye."

Chuck blows him off. "That's ridiculous. How would you know that from here?"

Steve sniffs again. "No, I'm serious. It's pastrami on rye bread." He pushes his nose tightly against the crack in the door. "Yes, and it's less than two days old—still very edible."

Chuck grabs his mouth. "That's sick!"

"Come on, let's go inside," Steve says, persuaded by the aroma of the food.

Stepping inside, the boys discover that the closet is not a closet at all. Instead, it is a huge room covered in dirt and filth from the ceiling to the floors. The lights are very dim, and they flicker with each step they take. The pitter-patter of little feet drift to their ears, running inside the walls.

"Mice!" Chuck exclaims, jumping onto Steve's back.

Steve dumps him onto the black, mucky floor. "Get off me, man! We're soldiers. We'll die in combat if we have to."

Chuck shakes his head. "No, we will not! I did not sign up for this. Let's find the janitor and get back."

Steve's eyes wander across the room, landing on the sandwich that is lying atop a desk beside a small cot in the corner of the room.

Steve's focus shifts to the sandwich, at which point nothing else matters to him. Chuck yells out something as Steve walks away, but his voice fades into a distant muffle, unheard by Steve with his concentration solely on getting the food. Steve moves in on the sandwich. With the sandwich firmly within his grasp, Steve opens his mouth wide, like a bass fish on a hook. Eyeballing the sandwich, just as he is about to take a delicious bite he feels something move inside the bread.

Chuck keeps his distance. Steve pulls the sandwich back from his face to give it another quick once-over before he decides to take a bite anyway. Another slight wiggle from the sandwich causes more concern for hungry Steve when—a little gray mouse pokes his head through the sandwich bread.

Steve drops the sandwich, "Aw, yuck! That's disgusting!"

Chuck slips on the muck from the floor, nearly losing his balance from laughing so hard. "I tried to warn you."

Steve jumps on the cot and begins hopping up and down, encouraging Chuck to join him. Chuck looks on as Steve continues hopping up and down, side to side, on the small cot that is barely big enough to fit one person for a comfortable night of rest. *Cling!* Steve's feet rip through the mattress, rendering him stuck. Imagine that—165 pounds of soft flesh hung up in the coils of a small cot in the spooky, dirty dark janitor's closet at ten o'clock in the morning on your first day of school. What a terrible situation to be in!

Steve pleads, "Chuck, help me. Don't just stand there. Do something! Get me free!"

Chuck rushes to Steve's aid, pulling at his legs that are sunken deep into the mattress. "Your legs are stuck, man. There's nothing we can do."

Steve leans back onto the mattress, pulling at his lower body with all his might, with Chuck tugging him from under his arms.

Wiggling and twisting as if it were an Olympic sport, Steve manages to break free of the springs. Chuck stands from the bed, with sweat beads cropped together on his forehead from the wrestle. He allows Steve to pull himself free of the mattress.

Turning his attention toward a concealed door in the room, Chuck hears faint voices in another room. Chuck calls Steve to follow him, moving in cautiously toward the door. "Steve."

There is no answer. He tries again. "Steve."

Still no answer, so he looks back, only to find Steve curled up asleep on the bed. Chuck smacks his head for the fourth time this morning, "Not again."

From the distant room, the voices get increasingly louder, and louder, and LOUDER, until Chuck must find out what is in the other room. This is a real pickle, leaving Chuck to make a decision quickly. Should he satisfy his curiosity and find out what is in the other room? Should he leave his friend asleep on the bed and take a chance on getting caught? Or should he awaken Steve so they can find the janitor and get back to class?

"What the heck," Chuck says, opening the door to the other room. "Dad says you only live once."

The door opens into the bleachers of the cold, gray gymnasium, with row upon row of metal seats going all the way up to the rafters. On the other side, a big, muscular man sits humped over alone, whistling a tune, pausing momentarily to talk to himself, then whistling the same tune again. Chuck finds the lonely, estranged man in the open empty gym a peculiar sight.

At first the man does not notice Chuck, but with the cold air surrounding him at every turn and with every breath, he sneezes. The man looks up to see the boy watching. Quickly, Chuck scurries back to the room.

Chuck dashes over to wake Steve up from his sleep, shaking him, shoving him, and lifting his legs in an attempt to awaken him. Nothing happens! In one last attempt at waking him, Chuck sits on his stomach— maybe not such a good idea, as a long squishy fart *warp!* comes from Steve's buttock.

Chuck pinches his nose. "Oh my gosh! What skunk just died?"

Thinking back to Mr. Rowe in the classroom and how he got

Steve awake, Chuck looks down at the sandwich on the floor and gets an idea. He squats down, picks up the sandwich—nearly throwing up his breakfast in the process at recalling the sight of the mouse in between the bread. He waves the sandwich in front of Steve's face. After a couple of waves across his nose, Steve comes to his senses, taking a plug out of the sandwich in a reaction to the smell. Steve, too, remembers the mouse in the sandwich and spits the bite of bread and meat to the ground.

Chuck informs Steve that they have overstayed their welcome. "Steve, we've got to go."

Steve strokes his eyes, not understanding what is going on. "No we don't; we just got here."

Chuck moves toward the door by the stairwell. "Yes we do. You've been asleep for a minute. I'll give you the details on the way back. Let's just get out of here."

Steve refuses to leave. "But we didn't accomplish what we came here to do. It'll still be freezing in the classroom if we leave."

Chuck digs around, looking for pen and paper on the cluttered desk beside the bed, while urging Steve to move toward the door. He finds what he is looking for, and then when he hears the hard steps of the grown man's boots clanging against the metal bleachers as he climbs up to the room.

Chuck scribbles on the piece of paper, "Please turn on the heat for Mr. Rowe room A-19," and races frantically out of the room, leaving Steve behind. Steve grabs a crumpled up bag of chips lying beside an open soda can and proceeds to stroll out of the room, his confidence still in tact.

Chapter Seven

Serena and Me

Ever so slowly, the big round clock on the wall ticks away the minutes, dragging the day out into an intolerable waiting game. With the first day of school nearly at an end, the children wait anxiously for the alarm that will bring the last period to a close. In Mr. Rowe's class, the seating arrangements have changed from the earlier homeroom and first hour periods as several of his students from earlier in the day have returned for the last hour period. Among them are Steve, Chuck, Sammy, and Ieka, Ms. Elle, the diva, has long gone from the premises, retiring for the day at the lunch hour. That annoying sound of the tick-tock, tick-tock, tick- tock is just about to drive Steve mad when *ring!*— the bell sounds.

Kids pour from the classrooms in all directions, flooding the hallways with loud screaming, the squeaking of sneakers against the floor, and the assistant principal rushing everyone to their appropriate bus. On his way to the bus, Chuck notices the most beautiful girl he has ever laid eyes on. She is in her own right a goddess of loveliness, with bold facial features giving her such a unique appearance that she could hardly be missed.

Ieka waits for her in the doorway. Struck by the love bug, Chuck walks away from Steve, veering from their route to the bus stop toward the meeting up with Ieka and the girl.

Steve does not notice Chuck's absence at first, but quickly realizes he will be riding the bus by himself if he doesn't catch Chuck. Steve yells out, "Chuck! Chuck! Where are you going?"

Chuck pays him no mind, as his eyes are locked on the beautiful girl with a long flowing ponytail, pearly white teeth, and the posture of a runway model. She is wearing a short, pleated skirt, a v-neck vest with a baby white tee underneath, and gleaming white kicks. Judging from her height and body, she has to be older—maybe eight grade or even the ninth. In any case, she has instantly won over the heart of the mighty Charles Rodriguez III, who has sworn off showing attention to any girls until he goes to college. But this one is different; she has a style that is intriguing to Chuck, luring him to her as if she is a booby trap.

Steve sprints in warp speed, interrupting Chuck's meeting the girl, all in the name of keeping him from losing his new best friend.

"Chuck, wait!" yells out Steve, as in slow motion Chuck's hand slides into the hand of the girl.

The girls stand there, listening, while Chuck stumbles over his words. "Hi, I'm Charles, I mean Chuck, but you can call me Chuckie—that's what my mom calls me," Chuck says to the girl, with her face turning red from embarrassment.

"OK, Chuckie. I'm Serena." Chuck holds her hand tightly, with his hands getting clammy from the excitement and sweat off his body.

"You mean like as in Serena Williams, the tennis pro?"

She smiles, nodding her head. "Yes, if only we were related. She's my idol; she's the best the game has ever seen." She looks at her sister, who is looking on. "I guess you've met my younger sister, Ieka."

He responds, "We have class together."

Given that Chuck acts older than he is, she is surprised to learn that he and Ieka are in the same class. "Oh, I didn't realize you were so young."

Chuck's response is "Age is just an irrelevant number."

Finally, Steve makes it over to them, trying to cover up that he is nearly out of breath. "Wait, Chuck. You don't want to do that."

Chuck looks puzzled, "Do what?"

Steve points to Chuck, who is still holding the girl's hand. "That."

Chuck reacts by looking at the girl, who is flattered at the attention. "I'm sorry." He looks over to Steve with a mean eye, then back at Serena. "Serena, this is my friend Steve."

Standing from lacing up her shoes, Ieka interrupts. "All right, enough with this. Are you ready to go, Re Re?"

She nods her head. "Bye, boys. Nice meeting you, Chuckie." She and Ieka walk through the front door of the school and off into the distance.

Chuck, love-struck and with gooey eyes, punches Steve in his arm with excitement. "Did you hear that? She called me 'Chuckie!'"

Steve shirks him off. "Yeah, and? So does your mom."

Chuck spins in circles. "You don't know anything."

Steve steps back to digest what Chuck has just told him. "I know that girls have cooties."

Chuck sighs. "Steve, that's so immature! Grow up, dude!"

Steve butts in. "OK then, how old do you think she is?"

Chuck ponders that for a minute. "I don't know—15, 16 maybe. Man, she's a hottie! My girl's a hottie!"

Steve nearly jumps out of his shoes. "What? How can you call her your girlfriend! You just met the girl, and already she's your girlfriend?"

With pride Chuck says, "Of course she is; we're in love."

Steve exclaims, "You *can't* be in love; you don't even know what love is."

Chuck sharply replies, "I do so know what love is. My dad loves my mom, and my mom loves him back. Once or twice a week my mom wakes up really happy in the morning, with a big smile on her face, and is really nice all day. My dad says he loves her and we have a big dinner that night. We'll be just like my mom and dad; just you wait and see."

The big yellow "boat of fun" pulls up at the stop, but the day has taken a strong turn in a different direction from the way it started out. Steve steps on the bus, unsure of where his friendship with his new best buddy is heading now, after the interference of Serena. His conversation is limited as Chuck watches the trees pass while he gazes out of the window, preoccupied with thoughts of the brown-eyed tennis princess.

For some reason, the bus does not have the same high energy it had in the morning when Steve first stepped on. Maybe everyone is tired from the first day of school; maybe the gloomy clouds looming overhead have everyone in a bad mood, but it seems that many of the children are not even on the bus for the afternoon route.

Steve brings this to Chuck's attention. "Chuck, is it me, or are there less people on the bus this afternoon?"

Chuck looks around, "Probably. Maybe most of them are involved with some sort of extracurricular activity."

Steve seems wowed. "Oh yeah? Like what?"

Chuck is still distracted and looking through the window. "Who knows? Football, baseball, tennis—I mean there are ton of things to get into."

The bus pulls up to their stop. Steve and Chuck rise from their seats and begin walking to the folding front door. As they step from the bus, Steve stops Chuck. "So why aren't you doing any of those activities?"

"It's simple; we don't have the money," Chuck shrugs him off.

Good ol' Mr. English stops the boys just before they step off. "Laddies, I will see you in the morning, bright and early. Be sure to be wearing your smiley faces. Now you lads run along and enjoy the rest of your day!"

Chapter Eight

Tough Boys Ain't Fast

As the boys exit the bus, in the distance they see three older boys top the small hill like giant walking trees. Rumor has it that Junior Brady—an all- around flunky—and his posse drift from neighborhood to neighborhood, wreaking havoc on every child in their path. The rumor has grown to legendary status since it first started nearly two years ago. It is said that they will casually walk up to you, demanding your money and anything they consider valuable. Junior's prey are middle-school kids, where he stands as a giant. In reality, he is only an average-size kid who is in his sophomore year of high school.

Junior and his crew continue in the direction of Steve and Chuck, who are unknowing of the dangers they are about to face. The other unsuspecting kids soon find that the horrible rumors are true. A loud scream comes from some girls ahead, stopping Steve in his tracks.

"Did you hear that?" Steve asks Chuck.

One little girl is lifted into the air, kicking and screaming, while one of the big boys fumbles through her pocketbook, taking her cash.

Chuck begins to tremble. "It's them."

Steve shakes Chuck. "Them who?"

"The Junior Brady Posse. I didn't think they actually existed. I thought it was all just a cleverly devised rumor. But it's true; they're here in real life—in the flesh."

Steve becomes agitated. "What are you talking about?"

Chuck picks up the pace, trying to lead Steve into a different direction. "They are the infamous gang that goes from hood to hood, robbing unsuspecting kids of their money."

Steve reacts. "That's foul! Why hasn't anyone done anything?"

Chuck looks over his shoulder to see if he's losing them. "They're too big."

Steve asks Chuck, "You really like that girl, huh?"

Chuck replies honestly, "What's not to like? She's pretty, smart, athletic, and she's feeling me. I hear her mom works at the candy factory too." Chuck makes sure to pick the pace up, suspecting that the bullies might mess with them once they were done with their current prey.

Steve shrugs his shoulders. "I don't know. I don't think I understand this girl thing. Girls are so simple; all they do is gossip, dress up and paint their faces. They don't do anything good like Xbox or something."

The sun seems to tilt on its axis, shining blaring hot rays at the boys who are trying to make it home without any confrontation. Though their houses are close by, the walk is longer today, with the goon squad beating up kids and taking their possessions just at the hilltop.

As the boys walk, Steve breaks the silence. "Do you think

you can get free candy if you go with her?"

Chuck laughs. "Maybe, but you need to layoff the candy before all your teeth rot in your mouth and just fall out at one time."

"That can't happen. Besides, I still have all of my teeth for your information," Steve replies with attitude.

The gang continues posting the kids up, reaching into their pockets and purses, taking whatever they please. They are finished with the first group of kids, and they head in the direction of Steve and Chuck.

Pointing toward them, Chuck sees trouble coming. "Oh yeah, well we had better get going unless you want to lose a few of them today."

Steve agrees, hurrying toward their houses, with the boys hot on their trail. Their pace increases more to a fast-paced walk, with Steve breaking a sweat from the humidity and sudden exercise. Out of shape, Steve pauses to take a break, with the big kids gaining ground on them with every step.

Chuck looks back to see Steve bent over, out of breath. "Steve, come on before they make lunch meat out of us! We're almost home!"

With his arms propped against his knees, Steve hangs his head through his legs only to see the kids who are much larger than them approaching—very fast. He pops up from his break, full of energy from his second wind. "OK, let's go." Walking as absolutely fast as they can, Steve breaks into a sprint, full of panic.

Suddenly the clouds appear as if they drifted down from heaven and settled on the ground, surrounding each of Steve's steps. The wind rushes behind his back and pushes him like a human kite into the air. Steve's body becomes weightless and free, allowing him to move effortlessly through time and space. The hot, beaming sun becomes his friend, feeding him energy like the photosynthetic cells of the leafy green plants. For only a moment, time stands still and all sound fades to nothing, letting Steve become totally free.

Appearing from nowhere is the familiar face of the old bearded man in his dream. Confucius says, "Steve, in the face of your confrontation, bold actions fend off intimidation better than your fist ever can. Develop confidence in your inner strength, your wit, and your mind to gain power over your enemy. You are stronger than he is; he just doesn't know it yet. Use the power within you, and your reward will be lifelong satisfaction of his defeat, stripping him of his power over you. Remember, no fear."

Chuck pushes Steve, who is struggling behind him with a big smile, wobbling from side to side like a penguin with his eyes closed. "Steve! Wake up! Snap out of it before they catch us!"

Steve opens his eyes only to realize that he is not flying, time is not standing still, and for some reason the old man likes to talk in riddles that he expects him to figure out.

In the horizon, the old railroad tracks that grace the entrance of their street is a welcoming site to see, for Steve and Chuck are trying to escape the clutches of evil.

Chuck begins a light jog, with Steve trailing closely behind. Though Chuck is much faster, he doesn't want to run off and leave his best friend. The big boys begin running also, leaving Chuck and Steve to resort to running at an all-out sprint, with the loose gravel chunks slipping below their feet when suddenly—*flop!* Steve crashes to the ground, with a sharp rock piercing his hand. With the crew catching up quickly, Chuck helps Steve up from the ground.

The boys continue running. Seeking a shortcut, they run through the brilliant rose garden of Mr. Osaki. Mr. Osaki is an introverted man, not very well known by his fellow neighbors, but familiar to the boys. He stands draped in a shiny red silk robe over his white karate outfit and wearing an old pair of leather sandals as he waters the carefully groomed rose bushes that proudly line the side of his home. The boys wave at him, racing past him and knocking a few of the rose petals to the ground, stretching with all their might to reach their home.

Steve pushes hard, running as fast as he possibly can. It's only 20 feet from the house, and the big kids are catching up fast! 15 feet from the doorway of safety of Chuck's house, but the bullies are closing on them! 10 feet, 8 feet, 5 feet. . . Chuck breaks away from Steve, sprinting to the house and screaming back to Steve, "Keep running! They ain't fast enough to catch us!"

Steve, trailing closely behind, plops belly first on the thickly painted old wooden porch, leaving the big brutes at the curb. It is a truly narrow escape for the boys, but a new concern to add onto all their experiences with their first day of school.

Chapter Nine

Lovebug Blues

The next day of school rolls around fast, with the kids hardly having time to comb their hair and brush their teeth before they are back in class again. Mr. Rowe steps to the front of the class, while the students take their seats for homeroom roll call. The class is unusually cooperative, to the surprise of Mr. Rowe, who is just waiting for something to happen. Today is particularly awkward, as the laughter shared amongst the group just yesterday has dwindled with Chuck's preoccupation with Serena. Mr. Rowe asks the class to get back into their groups and to continue working on the class project he assigned the day before.

Mr. Rowe notices an unopened pack of his favorite chewing gum lying on his desk. He smiles, thinking that one his students must be making a polite gesture to get on his good side. He addresses the class. "Excuse me, class. I'm not sure who left this chewing gum on my desk, but I would like to thank you for such an act of consideration."

The class looks puzzled. Mr. Rowe returns to his seat.

Placing their chairs into a circle, everyone notices the change in Chuck's participation. After finally having enough, Ieka asks, "OK, Chuck, what is the deal with you?"

Steve blurts out, "He's been bitten by the lovebug."

She laughs. "The lovebug for who? Re Re?"

He snaps back, "You shouldn't call her Re Re. That makes her sound retarded."

She rolls her eyes. "Let me tell you something, don't you tell me what I should or should not do with my own sister."

Chuck opens his mouth, but Steve quickly cuts him off. "Yes, he's hooked on Re Re—or Serena, or whatever her name is!"

Ieka laughs even harder. With Chuck's face turning beet red and fire rising in his eyes, Chuck addresses Ieka. "What is so funny about that?"

Ieka defends herself. "Nothing. It's just that Serena doesn't go for your type."

Chuck gets up from his seat. "Oh yeah? What type is that?"

Ieka stands to her feet directly in front of him, showing her superior size. "Non-athletic brianiac losers."

Chuck's face drops to the floor with the disappointing blow to his ego.

Ms. Elle makes an attempt to save face. "Cheer up, Chuck. I'm sure it can't be all bad!"

Chuck lays his head across his desk, with his arms hanging limply over the edge. For once, even Steve is at a loss for words, while Ieka continues writing on her tablet as if she never said anything at all.

Ms. Elle turns to Ieka. "Don't you feel the least bit sorry? Look at him! He's crushed, and it's all because of you."

Ieka pays her no attention, but continues to write on the yellow pages. "He's crushed because he likes my sister, who doesn't like him back."

Steve's eyes open wide as he notices Mr. Rowe starting to wiggle in his seat. "Don't worry, Chuck. I've got just the thing that will cheer you up." He points in Mr. Rowe's direction. "You see Mr. Rowe starting to squirm around? It's because that chewing gum is a laxative. I switched out the packaging to trick Mr. Rowe into taking it."

Sammy adds, "He's in big trouble. I think he ate two pieces."

Ieka nearly falls out of her seat, bursting out in laughter.

Mr. Rowe stands to calm Ieka down, but grips his stomach instead, hurrying out of the room. "Class, keep working. I'll be right back."

Quickly the word spreads around the room, and all the kids are in laughter, awaiting Mr. Rowe's return. Steve, with a smile a mile long, stands in front of the class taking a bow as all the kids cheer him on. Everyone is having a good time but Chuck, who is stuck on the fact that Serena does not like his type. Chuck makes up his mind that he is going to change Serena's type, even if it kills him.

The class settles back into their groups, and Steve returns to his seat, giving high-fives along the way. Sinking back into his seat, Steve is pleased with himself for bringing such joy to the faces of his fellow classmates at the teacher's expense.

Ms. Elle attempts to scold Steve. "Steve, how could you do such a thing to Mr. Rowe? That was a terrible thing to do."

Ieka speaks up. "Yeah, but you've gotta admit, it was funny!"

Ms. Elle breaks her serious face and they all break into laughter, even Chuck.

Ieka taps Chuck on his shoulder. "That's more like it. Lighten up, Pretty Boy. I'll tell you what. If it makes you happy, I'll set you up with her cell phone number, but the rest is up to you."

Chuck's head rises from his chest and his demeanor takes on new life. "You would do that for me?"

Ieka settles back into her seat calmly. "Of course I would. That's what friends are for."

Steve frowns, seeing past Ieka's smoke screen. "How much, Ieka? Nothing's free."

She smiles.

Mr. Rowe returns to the room, a stressed expression on his face. Just as he is about to retake his seat, he turns around immediately, grabbing his butt and dashing out of the room without having the chance to utter a word. The class goes completely wild! Steve is *the man*! No one has ever made a teacher leave the room twice in the same day; it's a new school record!

Ignoring the cheers and chants, Steve stares at Ieka squarely in her eyes. "How much Ieka? What's it going to cost Chuck for this supposed date?"

Her eyes lift from the pages of the yellow pad. "Ice cream after school at the corner store on Gracie Avenue."

Steve ponders for a moment. "Wait! Who are you really helping— him or yourself?"

She shrugs. "A little of both."

Chuck responds, "I don't have much choice. I'll do it. Just name the time. I'll be there."

Ieka sticks out her hand for Chuck to shake on the deal, but Steve quickly interrupts. "Wait! The phone number first."

She jots the number down on the tablet and rips a piece from the page. "Here, are you happy?"

Chuck takes the paper and shakes her hand. "Very."

Mr. Rowe creeps into the classroom, slowly walking as if he is trying to keep from awakening a hibernating bear. The pained expression on his face is so serious that instead of laughter, it brings sympathy from the class. The tables have turned, and now Steve looks like the bad guy.

RINGGGGG! The bell sounds, saving Steve from catching

the backlash of his cruel prank. Chuck leaves the room, happily staring at the piece of paper in his hand with Serena's number on it. Steve tails behind, disappointed with Chuck. Just before the kids exit the room, Mr. Rowe musters up the strength to shout out, "Children, don't forget that your group assignments are due on Monday! If you're not finished, I encourage you to talk over the weekend!"

Chapter Ten

Friendship Is Priceless

Stepping from the bus, Steve quickly looks around in search of the bullies of the Junior Brady Posse. With the coast clear, Steve and Chuck walk toward the house. Climbing from a black Ford Taurus is Sammy, only a couple of driveways away. Steve screams out, "Sammy! Hey, it's us!"

Sammy turns to the boys, concealing his excitement. "Hey, my friends," Sammy speaks shyly.

The boys run up to Sammy before he enters the house. Steve calls him to the front porch. "Sammy, come out and play with us."

Sammy shakes his head, disagreeing. "I cannot, I must do work now."

Chuck asks, "What work?"

Sammy replies, "Work for the home."

Steve sighs. "You mean homework? Relax! It's only the first week of school. Our only assignment is Mr. Rowe's."

A tall, slender man with a bulging round gut and thin gray hair steps to the door. He tells the boys, "Sammy, you can play with your new friends until supper. Then you'll have to come in." He goes back inside, leaving the boys on the porch to chat amongst themselves.

Steve questions Sammy. "Hey man, your dad is not Indian?"

Sammy shakes his head. "This is my exchange family." Sammy tucks himself into a small corner on the porch.

Steve picks up a baseball that he sees lying in the corner, tossing it to Sammy, but instead of catching it, he ducks.

Steve nudges Sammy on his shoulder, trying to help put him at ease. "Dude, you have to chill out! You're too uptight. Have some fun with us. Have fun while you're here!"

Chuck adds, "You are a little on the tense side. Steve's right; you have to open up if you want to hang with us."

Sammy is confused, "I'm sorry."

Chuck stands up, pulling Sammy from the ground. "Don't be sorry.

Look at that big, blue sky. There's a whole world out there waiting for us."

Steve jumps up. "And we're going to get it!" They form their hands into a circle, and with a little chant they throw them into the air. Steve looks around, "I have it!"

Chuck reaches for Steve's neck as if he would choke him. "Not again! I'm not going through this again."

Steve smiles. "No really, here's the deal. We already have the three of us for the class project; all we need is Ieka and Ms. Elle. We can meet up at say, the new museum downtown, and get the project done."

Chuck nods in agreement, "That's not a bad idea. I have Ieka's number."

Sammy pulls a piece of paper from his pocket, "I have Ms.

Elle's phone number." Continuing in his broken English, Sammy says, "She say she want to play my flute." Giving each other high-five's, Steve and Chuck pat Sammy on his back.

Steve replies, "Sammy, I didn't know you were a player."

Sammy smiles, "Oh yes, I play many instruments."

Chuck laughs, "OK, we'll work on that later. Let me have the number."

Reaching for the number, Chuck knocks over Steve's bag and out comes the broken picture frame.

Chuck thinks he is responsible for breaking the frame. "Steve, I think I broke your frame, man."

Steve responds, "Nah, I broke it yesterday."

Sammy asks, "You want me to throw it away?"

Steve quickly reacts. "No! I'm gonna get it fixed. I *have* to get it fixed."

Chuck looks at Steve. "It must be hard, dealing with a single parent mom. I can't imagine that."

Sammy shrugs his shoulders. "Me either."

Steve looks at both of his friends, whose eyes reflect nothing but sympathy. "Yeah, I miss my dad sometimes, but if it makes them happy, what can I do?"

Trying to fit the pieces of the frame together, Chuck asks, "But do you think they're happy?"

Steve takes a piece of the frame from him. "I don't know. My mom is so busy I hardly see her. I don't know what's going on." He pauses. "You guys wanna hear something strange?"

Sammy gets excited. "Yes, yes, please."

Chuck, suspecting a trap, cuts Sammy off, addressing Steve with a serious tone. "OK, but no smelly farts or funny business." The boys break out into laughter as Chuck's tone drizzles into a playful suggestion.

Steve's countenance changes. "This morning I had this dream, and this old man named Confucius came to me. It was so real! And he told me my job was to reunite the stone. What do think that means?"

Sammy adds, "Confucius? He was Asian!"

"A great philosopher to be exact, well respected in his time and responsible for a doctrine based on more than scientific principle," says Chuck. He continues, "Sounds to me like the stone is referring to the stone frame containing the picture of your and your family."

Steve shakes his head in agreement. "That's what I think, too."

Chuck interrupts. "But there's more; the stone frame is merely a metaphor for the greater concern." He puts the frame together, with the picture placed behind it. "Here! Looking deeper than the surface of the broken frame, you can see it clearly represents the reuniting of your family. That's certainly what he meant. It's your task to bring your family back together."

Steve looks at the broken frame in awe. "Wow! That's deep!"

Chuck places a call to Ieka and Ms. Elle, who agree to meet at the Museum of Science and Natural Arts at noon on Saturday. With everything falling into place, the boys begin seriously working on the project. Chuck gives each of the boys a topic to work on for the class presentation. Steve's lips turn up like a used dollar bill as he scrolls through his mind, trying to think of how to best work his topic into the presentation.

All of a sudden Sammy jumps up from the floor of the porch and races inside. He comes back out with a long gray keyboard, places it on the floor and begins to play, while writing in intervals on the tablet. Steve and Chuck are amazed at Sammy's talent.

Steve blurts out, "Hey, Sammy! You're really good at that keyboard."

Chuck adds, "You're very talented. I'm glad you're on our team. What else can you play?"

Sammy smiles, he starts playing Nelly's "It's Getting Hot in Here." The boys jump to their feet and begin dancing.

Sammy's dad comes to the door when he hears the music; he walks out onto the porch and begins dancing with the boys. In his enjoyment, he shouts out, "Let's get *Jiggy With It*!" For a second, the singing from the kids ceases. They look at each other in confusion, then start singing again. Steve takes his shirt off, exposing his big belly, which is tucked tightly inside his undershirt. Caught in the moment, Steve swings his shirt around over his head. The music comes to an abrupt halt and everyone stops, as Steve's breasts jiggle from side to side in the constraints of the undershirt.

Chuck cries out, "Steve, that's just gross! Put your shirt back on!"

They all laugh and begin to dance around again. They are having a great time, dancing to and fro, singing at the top of their lungs, with Sammy's dad, Gus. They continue until the remaining rays of the sun fade into the sunset, leaving the boys to retire to their own houses.

The next day, around eleven o'clock, Chuck shows up at Steve's door and bangs on the metal screen door.

Steve comes to the door in his Spiderman pajamas, rubbing the sleep from his eyes and sees Chuck and Sammy standing before him. "What are you guys doing here so early? I thought we said noon," Steve says, looking back at the clock. "It's only 10:59."

Chuck replies, "It's going to take us at least 40 minutes to get there, and you still have to take a shower and get ready. Look, tell your mom you're riding with us and she can pick you up around three."

Steve thinks it over of a brief second. "What about adult supervision?"

Chuck smiles as he and Sammy walk away. "Got it covered. Sammy's dad is supervising us and—Serena's gonna be there! Meet us at Sammy's in 20 minutes, and don't be late!" Chuck and Sammy race down the street, out of sight, leaving Steve at the door.

Steve walks up just as the old Ford station wagon pulls out of the drive, with the boys inside.

Sammy rolls down the window, wearing a big smile, "Come, get in. You sit beside me."

Steve climbs into the backseat of the car, where dirty mud-crusted shoes and yellow-stained, smelly socks line the car's interior. Steve pinches his nose as he sits down. "Boy, your dad must work really hard."

The father overhears him, "The name's Gus. I'm Sammy's exchange dad. You're right, little man. I'm a landscaper, and it is a lot of hard work." Pulling up at the stop sign, he turns to the backseat. "Say, it was nice meeting you boys last night. I hadn't moved that much in years. It was a lot of fun."

Chuck speaks up. "Yeah, I had fun too."

Steve adds, "Me too!"

Sammy screams out with excitement, "Me three!"

They continue driving until they reach the museum, where other parents are waiting with their children for the doors to open. There, in an all- white skirt and fresh white kicks, is Serena, looking like a goddess or an angel from the heavens, waiting by the fountain with her sister.

Chapter Eleven

Mystery of the Early Bird

The boys get out of the car, climbing over Steve, who looks discontent as he watches the other children arrive at the museum with their parents—especially the boys who are with their fathers. Chuck pulls Steve from the car, leaving Sammy's dad behind as they skip to the open entrance of the museum. The long steel doors remain closed, as dozens of children wait with their parents, brothers, sisters or guardians to enter into the place of fun and mystery. Steve and Chuck walk toward Serena and Ieka, while Sammy stands staring at a sign that is posted midway on the entrance door. The sign reads "Catch the Early Bird (before 11-12 pm); only $5.00 for children, $7.00 for adults. All entries $10.00 after 12."

Sammy rushes up to Steve, who is meddling in Chuck's

conversation with Serena. Sammy tugs at Steve's arm. "Steve, we must hurry if we want to catch the early bird!"

Steve looks at him without a clue. "What early bird? What are you talking about, Sammy?"

Sammy points at the sign. Steve gets it, and decides to play a prank on poor unsuspecting Sammy. Looking down at his wrist, Steve's watch shows it is ten minutes till twelve. He walks over to Chuck, interrupting him. "Chuck, we'll be right back. Sammy and I are going to catch the early bird."

As Steve and Sammy sprint toward the smooth, stainless steel doors that are reflecting the sun at high noon, they click open. The dozens of waiting children flood into the entrance, piling up at the admittance gate. Steve slips ten bucks from his pocket, passing it to the attendant behind his back as if it were a NBA pass to his favorite player, who happens to be LeBron James—a.k.a. King James.

Sammy asks, "Why do you pay when we don't have the early bird?"

Steve replies, "That's so we can catch him. Keep a close eye out; I know he's close by."

To Steve's amazement, a small bird has somehow found its way into the museum. The bird is so comfortable and familiar with the facility that it looks like it is right at home. The little bird hops across the floor, as Sammy's eyes light up like neon lights at the carnival. Sammy screams out, "There he is, there he is! Can you believe it?"

Steve, still in shock, says, "No, I can't. There cannot really be an early bird."

"But there he is!" exclaims Sammy. "Let's catch him."

Off goes Sammy, down the corridor, leaving Steve to trail behind him. The bird senses that he is being chased and scatters across the dull marble floor behind the Electromagnetic Terror Tunnel. Mistakenly, Sammy guides Steve into the tunnel where he thinks the bird has gone. Suddenly, the boys find their skin is tingly and their hair is standing on end. Steve's nappy fro straightens, while Sammy's hair stands straight up on end. As they move deeper into the tunnel, the lights dim and static pops from their clothing with every touch and every movement.

Sammy's amazement is evident from the enormous smile plastered across his face, while Steve stands by, looking in disbelief at the whole chain of events. Sammy touches Steve, and *pop!*— A little ball of static flares at the end of his fingertips, shocking Steve. Steve jumps. "Ouch! That stings."

He shocks Sammy back; Sammy likes the feeling. "Cool! Do it again." And again he does, with little lightening sparks filling the tunnel from the boys wrestling within.

The conveyor belt pulling them through the tunnel stops, and the bird hops across their path again. Sammy sees him. "Look, the early bird again!" He runs after the bird again, leaving Steve behind, trying to catch up with him. The bird is just within Sammy's grasp when he breaks into another run. Sammy and Steve chase him into the room, only to find that within seconds the doors clang shut.

Steve looks Sammy in the eyes. "Sammy, what have you gotten us into now?"

The boys stand with a few other children within the room of white padded circular walls with coarse soft rubber floors. Music fills the room; the anticipation of the kids builds. Steve peeks through a window of the room and sees the bird watching them from outside. A loud motor sounds from underneath them, and suddenly the walls begin to turn.

Sammy jumps on Steve's back, making him lose his balance and fall forward. As he does, something miraculous happens. Instead of hitting the floor, their bodies seem to defy gravity.

All the kids lift off the ground. The faster the walls spin, the higher into the air they float. This is amazing—totally unreal! Like the many dreams Steve has had of flying through the air, now it is actually happening. But what has he eaten that could have given him such powers? And if that were the case, why do Sammy and these other kids possess the same power? Maybe it is the room. Did they step into some sort of time warp or weightless portal? Simply amazing!

While the other kids play and tumble in the air, Steve reflects on his relationship with his father; he really misses him. He tells Sammy, "You know, Sammy, I know you're here only on exchange, but you're very lucky to have your dad around all the time."

Sammy sadly cowers behind his soft voice. "Yes, but it is not easy being an exchange kid. My exchange brother and sister hate me. They say I get all of the attention. I like them and I want them to like me, but they say mean things. . . That's no fun."

Steve looks through the window, seeing the top of the heads of the onlookers outside. A deep male voice speaks up from nowhere, calling out "Steve."

Steve looks past Sammy, who is doing mid-air flips into the glass, trying to see a familiar face.

Confucius says, "It is I, Confucius, with a message for you. I have endowed you with the ability of weightlessness. Though it is only for a brief moment, this insight should allow you to overcome your anxiety of height and fear of your weight. If man can accomplish flight, there is nothing you cannot achieve. Tap into your talents, put the snacks down, live long and be happy."

Swoosh! The fresh air rushes into the room that is sealed by the airtight doors. *Peep! Peep!* Sings the bird as he dances on the railing of the wheelchair ramp, mocking Sammy, who has tried so diligently to catch him. But Sammy doesn't give up so easily; he dashes from the room, with speed and agility on his side. Grabbing a McDonald's bag from atop the waste can, he hurries to dump the contents into the garbage before the bird hops away.

There it is! The bird perches on the branch of a small tree within the museum. In one fair swoop, Sammy makes a leaping dive, catching the bird.

With all the excitement, Sammy forgot that Steve was

nowhere to be found. He scampers back to the padded room and sees his father, standing above the unconscious Steve, who is lying on the floor.

Sammy hurries in. "Excuse me, I must wake him up; he's asleep." Sammy commences wildly smacking Steve's face while his father looks on in bewildered amusement behind him.

Sammy's father asks, "Sammy, are you sure he's asleep?"

Sammy snatches the cup of water from his father's hand, "Yes. See?" He pitches the water on Steve's face until he gasps for air. Sammy turns back to his father, "Told you he was sleeping. He's always very sleepy."

Steve, Sammy and Gus exit the museum, walking up to a picnic table where Ieka, Ms. Elle, Chuck and Serena await them. Chuck lifts his head from the table. "Hey guys, where have you been all this time? We're all done with the assignment. Serena and Ieka were about to go. We are just waiting on Ms. Elle's mom."

Sammy answers, "Inside!" He lifts a paper bag into the air. "Me and Steve caught the early bird!"

The kids laugh at Sammy's delight with the capture of the bird. Ms. Elle sits at the end of the table, alone and withdrawn.

Steve pulls away from all the commotion and approaches Ms. Elle with a sensitive side he rarely shows. "Hey, are you OK?"

She frowns, trying to hold back her tears of disappointment at her mother's tardiness—again. "Yeah, I'll be OK." Her lip starts to quiver as a tear drops from her eye.

Steve hands her a napkin from his pocket, anticipating her troubles. "Don't worry, she doesn't mean anything by it."

Wiping her tears, Ms. Elle turns to Steve in surprise. "What do you mean?"

Steve looks around to ensure that everyone is still entertained by Sammy. "Look, my mom picks me up late sometimes, too. Sometimes she helps me with my homework; other times she can't keep her eyes open long enough to finish

71

dinner, so I resort to TV dinners. Did you know they make them healthier now?"

She laughs, breaking the frown resonating on her face. He reaches out for her. She places her hand in his as they have a heart-to-heart conversation for being the children of single parent moms.

Steve continues. "My mom says nothing is constant—just constantly changing. I guess that means our relationships with our parents, too. My mom and dad are separated now. Who knows if they'll make up and get back together."

She replies, "Yeah, the same year we moved here, my dad was sent off to Somalia for a year and a half. When he came back, things between them wasn't the same and he moved out." She rests her head on his shoulder. "It's really hard, Steve, you know?"

Ieka looks up to see Ms. Elle's head on Steve's shoulder. She brings attention to their moment of discovery. "Hey, what are you guys doing down there?"

Steve jumps from his seat to protect himself, but more importantly to protect Ms. Elle from the teasing and taunting that would come if the kids were to learn about the subject of their conversation.

She understands Steve's reaction and plays along. "What are you talking about Ieka? I was getting tired and decided to rest my head on Steve's shoulder. Is there any crime in that?"

Sammy, still filled with excitement, runs up to his dad. "Me and Steve caught the early bird."

Sammy's dad winks at Steve, letting him know he is onto his joke. "Yes, you caught the early bird, did you, Steve?"

Ieka speaks up. "Let me see."

Sammy walks over and opens the bag, but there is nothing inside except a couple of napkins. Instead, a small hole is on the inside of the bag between the McDonald's golden arches where the bird escaped.

A bird's chirp comes from the fence that surrounds the

museum's parking lot. The chirp is from the early bird holding a worm, dangling from his mouth. Sammy's demeanor changes and he is suddenly saddened that he did not catch the bird.

Chuck adds a quick little joke to lighten the moment. "Guess it's true what they say: the early bird does catch the worm after all." They all laugh as they prepare to go their separate ways.

Steve's mom pulls up into a space in the parking lot and blows the horn. He signals her over to meet his friends. Stepping from the car, she apparently has just come from work, as she sports a pair of fitted scrubs with her hair pulled back into a ponytail. About the same time, Chuck's dad walks up from the opposite side of the parking lot toward the group.

Chuck smiles. "Looks like all the adults are here today."

Steve's mom walks up to the group. "Hi, guys! Are you ready, Steve? I have another appointment at five."

Steve sighs, "Everyone, this is my mom. I call her 'Super Mom' because she's always working!"

Only Ms. Elle laughs with Steve. His mom squeezes the back of his neck, letting him know she did not appreciate the joke. "It was nice meeting all of you. I'm sure we'll have the chance again soon," she adds, walking away, with Steve's wrist in her hand.

Chapter Twelve

Friends Say the Darndest Things

It's Monday morning, and school is back in session after a short weekend break. In Mr. Rowe's class, everyone seems rested and satisfied from their weekend. Everyone is eagerly anticipating the presentation of the class assignments. Chuck gives the finishing touches to the assignment, while his team sits back, proud and confident with the information they have collected about each other.

Mr. Rowe calls the first group before the class. They slowly drag themselves to the front of the room. It is obvious that they are not prepared for a presentation, and they ramble on for five minutes about nothing other than what they had for dinner on Saturday and how many shades of blue the sky had changed the day before with the approaching storm.

The next group is not much better, the only thing different they have to share with the class that Big Stinky's pet rabbit got hit by a car and died on the way to the veterinarian's office.

Chuck pulls his group together at the last moment, just before they are called to the front of the class. Chuck says with excitement, "OK, we have to do something different. Those guys stunk, and I don't mean 'cause of Big Stinky!"

The kids burst into laughter. Chuck quiets them. "I don't want to go up there and look stupid like them."

Ms. Elle questions, "What do you suggest we do?"

Chuck leans in and says, "I have a better plan."

Chuck and the group walk to the front of the room. Chuck addresses the class. "Today, class, we have a different spin on our assignment. Rather than just getting to know each other, we took the time to spend the day at the museum downtown on Saturday. We got to know each other in a different setting, but we also had the chance to meet each other's parents and siblings. Today we'd like to share with you our impressions of those people we met."

Mr. Rowe looks up from his desk, very pleased. "This should be good."

Chuck continues to address the class. "As the group leader, I'll begin. I had the chance to meet and talk with Ieka's sister, Serena."

Steve's eyes nearly pop out of his head as he smacks his forehead. "I can't believe this!"

Ieka and Steve stand behind Chuck in conversation. Ieka says, "I cannot believe he is talking about Serena. She is the subject of his report?"

Steve replies, "Yeah, it must have been his plan all along." Chuck continues sharing his impression of Serena with the class. "And what I like most about her is that she is so focused and knows where she wants to go, much like myself. But this is not the only commonality we share. . ."

Steve impolitely interrupts. "No, it isn't, and fortunately we all have experiences to share, or else you guys would have to hear about his obsession with Serena all day."

The entire class breaks into laughter, with Steve sharing a pound with Ieka at Chuck's embarrassment. Steve continues, "I got to meet Sammy's father. He's white!"

The class gasps. Sammy shyly steps behind Ms. Elle.

"I didn't expect a white guy to walk out of Sammy's house, but he's really cool. See, Sammy's not your typical foreign exchange student."

Sammy holds his breath, thinking Steve is going to divulge his secret, ruining any chance he would have at fitting in.

Steve glances over at Sammy. "No, he's really cool. We hung out at the museum, and I found out that deep down inside Sammy is a bird lover!"

The group snickers among themselves. Steve smiles, "And Sammy's dad told us to call him Gus. He's really a cool guy! He told us we are welcome to play with Sammy. He came out on the porch and danced with us, and then he even took us to the museum.

From the back of the room, Mr. Rowe interjects, "Sammy, it sounds like you have a really nice father."

Steve adds, "Oh, yeah, he's really nice, and he works hard. He's a landscaper and plants trees and grass at different buildings and houses."

Chuck adds, "He must really enjoy his job, 'cause when he met Steve's mom on Saturday, I heard him say he would really like to sow some seeds at her house."

Several kids in the class laugh, and Mr. Rowe's face turns beet red. Steve shakes his head in disbelief at Chuck's naive comments.

Chuck continues. "I think, though, if I worked that hard all week like Gus, I wouldn't want to sow seeds for anyone on the weekend. I'd have to take a break."

Mr. Rowe interrupts, replying, "A break—that sounds great. Class, we'll take a 3 to 4 minute break for those of you needing to go to the bathroom or get water. We'll resume where we left off when we return."

Steve turns to Chuck. "You're an idiot!"

Chuck looks puzzled as the rest of his group walks away. "Why? What did I do?"

Steve replies, "It's not what you did; it's what you said."

Chuck is still clueless. "What did I say?"

The class returns and Ieka stands in front of the class, speaking on behalf of the group. She stands upright and confident, like a politician, "Ok, look, I'm not sure what we were supposed to be doing, so I'm just gonna tell you what I saw. After Steve left, I met Elle's mom. She's nice, but she's just like Elle."

Ms. Elle stands quietly, but proud of herself and her mom.

Ieka continues. "Let me tell you, they must share a special bond, because are identically alike. Her mom is tall, thin, and very pretty, also." The compliments appear to err on the side of a set up, rather than a compliment.

Ieka's continues. "But she's got one big yellow tooth in the back of her mouth that shows when she smiles."

The class reacts with an "Ooooh!"

Ms. Elle's smile turns to a frown as Ieka continues with her report.

"That tooth must be decayed, because it makes her breath hot. I mean *really* hot!"

Ms. Elle reacts. "What?"

Ieka turns to her, staring her squarely in her eyes. "I don't stutter. Your mom's got some seriously bad breath!"

Ms. Elle feels the sense of urgency rushing through her body, wanting to stand up for her mom. "That's not true, take that back!"

Within seconds, they are in each other's face.

Chapter Thirteen

Nothing Like a Good "Girl Fight"

The group stands in front of the class as the girls move in closer to each other. Suddenly, the class starts cheering, "Fight! Fight! Fight!"

Before Mr. Rowe gets a chance to move from his seat, the girls are going at it! Ms. Elle proves to be a scrappy little fireball, giving Ieka all she can handle. Ieka throws a punch, then a jab, but Ms. Elle is too quick for her as she dances from side to side, like a skilled ballerina on ice.

Ieka's frustration shows in her face.

Steve screams, "Keep moving, Elle! Don't let her hit you! Her punch will drop you!"

Chuck backs him up. "Yeah, stick and move! Stick and move!"

Ieka grabs Ms. Elle's sweater, swinging her into the unsuspecting Steve, who is bent over lacing up his shoe.

Ms. Elle comes at Steve with such force that it knocks him to the ground. Steve jumps up. "Hey! That's not fair! I had nothing to do with any of this." He pushes Ms. Elle back into the fight. "Get in there and finish what you started!"

Ms. Elle steps back to the center of the classroom, now a sparring ring, with her much stronger opponent, but she keeps her cool. Swinging wildly at Ms. Elle, Ieka catches Mr. Rowe with a hard punch to the groin. He buckles, grasping for air, and waddles to his desk for a quick recovery. Ieka throws a punch that is sure to catch Ms. Elle in the stomach, but with a quick reaction, she grabs a book to protect her mid-section and deflecting Ieka's punch.

And so the fight goes on for nearly three minutes, almost a full minute longer than the record held by two previous 6th graders—Montez Spencer and Ronald Dickerson, a year ago—but never in history have two girls battled with such elite skill, sophistication, enthusiasm, and held their audience completely captive. Never have two girls been so equally matched that a fight could last as long as this one. Truly, this is no ordinary fight. They are not scratching and clawing like cats in a squabble. Instead, it is like the pipsqueak David meeting the giant Goliath. How could Ieka not win? She is bigger, stronger, and surely a better fighter than Ms. Elle. But like all Goliaths of the world, on any given day even the strongest can fall.

In the hallway, the noise is heard several feet away from Mr. Row's door. The principal just happens to be walking down the hall, doing a routine check, when she hears the commotion. She changes direction and walks toward Mr. Rowe's class, with a stern scowl across her face. Approaching the door, she pauses before entering.

With the most ironic timing, the shy kid, Sammy, gets in on the cheering. "Ieka must kick butt!" he yells as the principal walks in at that precise moment. The entire class bursts into laughter, while Sammy jumps up and down filled, with excitement.

Ieka looks over at Sammy and loses her concentration. She begins laughing, too. All of a sudden, *pow!*— Ms. Elle catches Ieka in the chin with a spinning roundhouse high kick. The giant falls to the ground in slow motion, just as Mr. Rowe makes his way to the front of the classroom for a second time.

With all of the excitement, he does not realize that the principal has walked in. He asks, "What happened?"

The class is wowed, but drifts into a silence with the principal amongst them.

Ms. Elle smiles confidently. "I knocked her out, compliments of two years of Tae Kwon Do." She does a squatting bow to the class, who applaud her, smacking high-fives with each other.

The principal walks to the front of the class. Mr. Rowe's eyes open wide, showing every centimeter of his white eyeballs. Little beads of sweat bunch up around his eyebrows, awaiting the words of guidance from his boss, Principal Winkleshire, affectionately referred to by the kids as "Principal Winkie."

She sternly addresses him. "Mr. Rowe, I just happened to be walking down the hallway when I hear this rather unruly noise coming from your room, and I walk in to find this. What do you have to say for yourself?"

Mr. Rowe stammers and stutters, trying to get his words out. "Mrs. Winkie. . ."

The class interrupts, blurting out into laughter, "Winkie! That's funny!"

The principal abruptly corrects him. "That's Winkleshire!"

Mr. Rowe corrects himself. "Yes, Principal Winkleshire. My apologies. This situation happened so quickly that I could not prevent it."

Mr. Rowe cowers behind his desk as he and Principal Winkie talk in private about what just happened and the appropriate decision for disciplining the two girls. Mr. Rowe's face flushes hot red as his glasses fog up, with the principal verbally blasting him in a soft tone as to not be overheard by the children of the class. Though the kids can't hear their conversation, her facial expressions say more than words could ever describe.

The kids sit like statues, in an awkward silence, out of fear for the commanding presence the principal demands. Although she is only in the classroom for five minutes, tops, it seems like a lifetime for Steve and the bunch who are anxious to discuss the excitement of the fight that occurred only moments earlier.

Suddenly the principal turns to the awaiting students. "Class, I am sorry that you had to witness such a lack of control on your teacher's behalf. For those of you who are serious about learning, I can assure you that it will not happen again."

She turns to address Ieka, whose eye is swelling at a rapid pace, and Ms. Elle, who is nursing her bruised knuckles. "As for you young ladies, you will have three weeks' suspension. Upon your return, you will have to present to me a five-page essay on the family history of each other."

Ieka reacts. "What?"

Ms. Winkie responds, "Excuse me?"

Ieka corrects herself. "I'm sorry, Ms. Winkleshire, but that doesn't seem fair. If we don't like each other, how can you expect us to be around each other long enough to get the information we would need to write a five- page essay?"

Ms. Winkie smiles. "Let's see, here. Well, I don't know, but then again that's not my problem."

Steve leans over, whispering loudly to Chuck in his ear. "Three weeks? Whew, that's harsh!"

Chuck replies, "Yeah! Ieka needs to just shut up and take the lighter punishment."

Sammy, never having witnessed such an ordeal, isn't quite sure what to make of it. He asks the boys, "What is going to happen to them? Are they going to jail?"

The boys laugh. Steve replies, "No, just a couple of days away from school, but I would hate to be at their houses tonight."

Chapter Fourteen

Eyes on the Prize

Thinking about the events from earlier in the day with the two girls fighting, he realizes that he was in that same predicament just a few days prior, escaping the clutches of Junior and his gang. Chuck sits quietly on his bed with his arm around his legs and his head resting atop his knees. He contemplates what he should do about the bullies who are destined to confront him after not having been able to catch him and Steve. Sure, several days have passed without a peep out of them, but it is well known throughout the neighborhood that they strike just when you least expect it.

Chuck's father walks into the room. "Charles, is something the matter? You didn't finish all of your mom's pasta, and that's not like you."

Chuck shakes his head as his chin sinks deep into his chest. His father continues, "Hey, buddy, look I'm your dear ol' dad. You can talk to me. So what is it, what's on your mind?"

Chuck is unresponsive.

Chuck's mom sees that her husband is unsuccessful in his effort thus far, and she walks in, offering to help. "Honey, is there something you want to tell us? Is it school? Or maybe it's that pretty girl I heard you talking to your friends about?"

Chuck looks up at his mom with big tears hovering in his eye ducts, just waiting to drop down his face any minute. "It's none of that. Don't worry about it; I'll have to handle it on my own."

His father suspects the problem. "I see. I think I know what it is." He looks at his wife and says, "Let me handle this, honey." Turning to Chuck, he caresses the back of his neck. "When a man has to take things into his own hands, that can only mean one thing: trouble. Son, trouble is a funny thing. It is incredibly easy to get into, but almost impossible to get out of."

Looking up from his knees, Chuck addresses his father. "You don't get it, Dad. These are real problems."

His dad keeps his composure. "Oh, but I do, son. See, you must realize that you come from a heritage of fine fighters."

Chuck's eyes pop open wide and his ears perk up at the mention of fighters, unaware of his father's perceptiveness.

His dad continues. "Ah, so I have your attention now. Yes, I said fighters. Son, there comes a time in every man's life when he must defend himself against evildoers and those who wish us harm. I would rather you use a peaceful means of resolving your problems, but if you must fight, you should know that your ancestors were warriors."

His mother looks disappointed in how the conversation is shaping up. "Charles, only use force when it is absolutely necessary and there are no other alternatives."

Chuck asks his dad, "Like who? Who were these great fighters?"

He responds, "Let's see, there was Manny Manuel, Pedro Vegas, Rico Gomez, and of course the all time great, Don Diego."

Chuck leaps up from his bed excitedly. "Wow!"

Chuck's mom adds, "Yes, honey, those men where all great fighters, but don't forget people like Caesar Chavez, who fought courageously without violence so that Hispanic farmers would have better wages, resulting in better opportunities for us today."

Chuck thumps his chin. "Like Martin Luther King?"

She replies, "Yes, he would be the Hispanic equivalent to Dr. King. Son, I just want you to remember that a fight does not always mean you have to use your fists; you can fight people with your mind and win."

Chuck's dad stands up from the bed. "Those great fighters I spoke of always fought for a prize. You want to know what that prize was?"

Chuck nods his head, and his dad continues. "A purse."

Chuck reacts with, "A purse?"

His mom politely covers her laugh as his dad continues to explain himself. "The 'purse' was the money at stake for the boxer's pursuit in the fight. The purse was often worth several hundred thousand dollars. Tell you what, if you manage to find a way to win your war on your own, I will make your purse a slice of that peach cobbler from the parlor around the corner you love so much."

Time seems to rush by as the days and nights stack on top of each other. Chuck has taken it upon himself to intensively train his body with sit -ups and pushups to tighten up his small frame. In the three weeks of Ieka and Ms. Elle's absence for suspension, Chuck gets himself prepped for the fight of his life. He researches the old classic fights online of Ali, Louis, Forman and Tyson, studying their styles and techniques.

Finally, the day has come. There they are, standing at the bus stop. Chuck could see the Junior Brady Bunch standing in their semi-circle, waiting to torment them as they exit the bus. Chuck tenses up and begins chanting to himself, "Eye on the prize, eye on the prize, eye on the prize."

Steve, unaware of the bullies awaiting them, asks Chuck what is going on with him. Chuck replies that he is focusing on his purse—whatever that means.

They step from the bus at 3:45. Like clockwork, the bully and his posse begin picking on the kids as they file out of the bus. One of the sidekicks is eating ice cream from a waffle cone, while he looks on at his bully friend, harassing the boys. With all the strength of the great warriors of his family before him, Chuck takes a step in front of Steve, who is in their line of fire. Chuck proclaims, "I am not going to take it any more. You should be on your way—or else."

Off in the distance, Steve sees their old Asian neighbor, Mr. Osaki, peeking at the scene with a watchful eye.

Junior laughs in his face, when suddenly. . .*pow!*— Chuck draws back and lays one on him, right in the smacker. Chuck kicks him in his shin. Junior hops up and down in pain. With two quick gut punches, Chuck brings the big brute crashing to the ground. Deciding not to wait until the much larger bully becomes angry enough to beat them to a pulp, the two boys decide to dash off for safety. Chuck feels satisfied with his temporary defeat, but he knows there will probably be repercussions of his actions to follow.

On their way home, Steve shares his discovery with Chuck. "Man, you really showed him! I don't know where that came from. I didn't know you had it in you. But while your where doing all that punching, you won't believe who I saw watching in the distance?"

Chuck asks, "Who?"

"Mr. Osaki," says Steve as he wipes the sweat from his brow.

"As in our neighbor, Mr. Osaki?" Chuck asks.

Steve slows down his pace. "Yes, he was watching us, but it

was like he was our very own guardian angel or something. I don't think he would have let anything bad happen to us."

Chuck sighs. "That's good to know, 'cause there's no telling what they'll do to us the next time we run into them."

Steve sighs. "I know; that's a big problem." They continue walking until they come to Mr. Osaki's Rose garden, but on this day the front door of his house is cracked. The boys become curious. Steve looks at Chuck.

"Look! The door is open. Should we pop in and say thanks?"

Chuck doesn't respond, but they walk up to the door with caution, looking to and fro for Mr. Osaki.

Chapter Fifteen

House of Mirrors

The boys step within the walls of the house. The room opens into an enormous space with high vaulted ceilings. Indeed, this could be the largest room within a house the boys had ever seen, but it is also the strangest. The walls are lined with pictures of Mr. Osaki in different colored robes and gowns. Each step they take is scarier than the next as more of the room becomes exposed.

Chuck leans into Steve's ear. "You know what? It's funny that you, Ieka and Ms. Elle's dads are in the military."

Steve reacts. "No, it's not. With the war going on, almost everybody is in there."

Chuck says, "Yes, but all of you have recently moved here, even Mr. Rowe. Doesn't that strike you as being a bit odd?"

Steve recognizes that Chuck is fishing for a reaction. "No, not really. Well, maybe. I don't know."

Chuck continues pushing Steve's buttons. "What if your dad might be involved in some secret mission to protect the Secretary of Defense or something?"

Steve gives a smug smile. "That's a little far fetched."

Steve thinks about it for a second. He is about fed up with Chuck. "I don't know what you're talking about, and you know what? I don't care. I'm ready to get out of here."

Chuck pushes him forward. "Come on, we just got here. Let's find out what we can see."

They move further inside, where they see mirrors nearly everywhere—small ones, big ones, long rectangular ones, and ones that look like clocks. Mirrors line the interior of the entire living room of the allusive Mr. Osaki. His house is decorated in an antique Japanese fashion, fitting what one would think to be customary in the days of the powerful Japanese rulers.

Chuck looks over at Steve and whispers, "This is like the House of Mirrors at the carnival."

Steve replies, "Yeah, but it's for real."

"Chirp! Chirp!" two parakeets intone from the dark corner of the room, almost giving Steve a heart attack and making Chuck nearly pee on himself. Chuck lashes out at the birds, "Shhh! You're going to give us away!"

From the distance, Mr. Osaki announces his presence. "Ah, come right in, boys. I've been awaiting your arrival."

Steve and Chuck look at each other apprehensively, wondering what they are about to step into.

Deep within the great house is a kitchen with an open-air roof, a brick island range, and a bar with four stools placed around it. At the left of the bar is a marble-top table, with Mr. Osaki sitting there calmly, drawing on a cigar. As the boys pull their seats up to the table, they notice the most peculiar thing: Mr. Osaki is sitting at the table, alone, with three teacups placed before them. From around the corner, a beautiful young Asian mistress walks up to the table and pours tea into each of their cups. She graciously bows, then turns and walks away with satisfaction.

The boys sit quietly, awaiting instruction from Mr. Osaki, not sure what to make of this occurrence. Drawing from the cigar, Mr. Osaki speaks. "Mirrors reflect who we believe we are, or at least what we see on the outside. A skillful opponent weakens his mark's defense by presenting the image he wants to see." He takes another draw from his cigar. "Boys, you're probably wondering why I have invited you into my home."

They nod their heads and he continues. "It's merely to invite you for a cup of tea."

They look at each other, confused. Steve responds, "A cup of tea? That's it? But what's with all the mystery and secrecy?"

Mr. Osaki leans forward, putting out his cigar. Smiling, he says, "In my country many great conflicts have been resolved over a mere cup of tea. It is the art of a gentleman showcasing his patience over his ego."

Chuck speaks up. "I'm sorry Mr. Osaki, but I don't understand. What does any of this have to do with us?"

Mr. Osaki picks up his cup, leans back in his chair and takes a sip of his tea. "Ah, this is good tea. Try some, please."

Chuck reaches for the cup. Taking a sip, he encourages Steve to try some too. Steve shakes his head. "No thanks. I like mine with sugar."

Mr. Osaki laughs. "No, son, this is not meant to be sweetened. It's an herbal elixir that purifies your mind and thoughts. After a few sips, you will think more rationally and clearly than you ever have before."

Chuck nudges Steve. "Come on, man, try some. Don't be a chicken. It's very soothing."

Steve tries some of the tea and smiles, showing that he actually likes it. Now that the boys are sipping the tea and enjoying his company, Mr. Osaki reveals the real reason he invited the boys there. He picks up the bud of the most perfect red rose, freshly picked from his garden, passing it to the boys.

Rising from his chair, Mr. Osaki calls the woman back into the room; she returns promptly. He continues. "Boys, allow me to formally introduce you to Mae Ling."

She stands before them, garbed in a long, flowing, white silk kimono, trimmed in lace, with intricate designs embroidered along the lace sleeves. Her appearance is as rigid as a statue, but her gracefulness is angelic while she awaits the reason she was summoned to the room.

Mr. Osaki directs his attention to Steve. "Young man, would you like to know who she is?"

Steve replies, "I don't know. Your daughter, maybe?"

He laughs out loud. "No, of course not. How old do you think she is?"

Steve answers, "I think about 25."

Chuck spurts out, "No, she's closer to 30."

Mr. Osaki reaches for his cup of tea, calmly taking a sip. He says, "She is my wife of 31 years, so let's see, that would make her 56."

The boys react. "What? No way! That's amazing!"

Chuck speaks up. "You must have the fountain of youth. What's the secret?"

After waving his wife away, Mr. Osaki retakes his seat. "The secret, boys, is in the tea. And the key to your happiness in life lies in that rose bud right in front of you."

By this time Steve is becoming irritated with the parables and ambiguous talk of Mr. Osaki. He blurts out, "What do you mean? All this stuff about tea and rose buds? I'm confused."

Mr. Osaki replies, "As you should be. Without guidance, a good seed falls on bad soil and bears no fruit. Let's take your friend Junior, for example."

The boys sit up in anticipation of what he is about to say.

Mr. Osaki continues. "He was once a good kid like you boys. He took an interest in the wrong crowd and began to disobey his parents. Before long he became a problem to his parents and the community. Unless he turns his life around, he will very likely end up in jail, on the streets without a home, or worse, maybe even dead."

Chuck wipes his head in relief. "I'm sorry, but if you're trying to scare us, my mom already gave me this talk."

Osaki lets Chuck finish, then picks up the rose bud. "This rose bud represents a woman. The secret of the beauty that lies within this bud is understanding its' nature. Like a woman, the garden from which this bud came must be constantly given affection and attention. It must be manicured to lure out the optimum beauty it possesses. And like a woman, the rose requires patience, understanding, compassion, and the constant struggle for tranquility to see the greatest results in the relationship you yield."

Steve hops up. "OK, that's it! Mr. Osaki has finally gone over the deep end!"

Chuck motions for Steve to sit back down. "No, wait a minute, Steve! He's on to something here. Please proceed, sir."

Mr. Osaki grins at Chuck's perceptiveness. "As for the secret in the tea, well it's not in the tea as much as it is the ceremony. Boys, I have a secret to let you in on. Many years ago, in my native land, I inherited the infamous Shao Lin teacup from my great-great grandfather, General Yao, a high ranking Japanese military official. Yao studied in the ancient art of the Tea Ceremony. Its concept is rather simple. You sit at a table with your adversary and discuss your differences or problems over a nice, civil cup of tea. The ceremonies date all the way back to the 1700s, when General Tso Tso conquered entire nations by working his magic with a cup of tea."

The boys sit, a cloud of confusion hovering above them. Osaki tries to clear up the confusion. "OK, let me put this in a practical example for you. When you boys race through my garden everyday, you upset the delicate balance of tranquility and harmony with the essential elements of the sun that I am trying to create for my roses. Rather than becoming upset with you, I choose to sit you down for intelligent conversation and share with you what is on my mind. This, my friends, is how the law of the Tea Ceremony works."

The boys finally get it, but in getting it, they also realize they have offended their dear neighbor. Steve acknowledges their wrong. "Mr. Osaki, if that's what all this is about, we are really sorry, and I promise we won't do it again."

He smiles. "Gratification and servitude."

The boys respond, "Huh?"

He says again, "Gratification and servitude. The first law of the ceremony is about gratifying one's self for something they would like to accomplish with the discussion. I wanted you to understand how I feel about my roses and wish to stop on your own accord. It's more effective than me forcing or coercing you to stop. The second law of the ceremony is about servitude; it's what set apart the mediocre Tea Masters from the best."

He reaches for the teapot, pouring himself another cup as he asks, "More tea?"

The boys get their cups refilled, as a wealth of knowledge unfolds before them.

"When I studied the ceremony under Yao, he taught me what balances the law is servitude; you must always give something for that which you have taken. If I want something from you, I will get better results if I have something to offer you in return, so you create a win-win scenario."

Chuck's forehead crunches up as he tries to grasp the concept. "A win-win scenario?"

"Yes," replies Osaki. "It is where both parties get what they want. It is the universal law to settling conflict."

"You are a very knowledgeable man, Mr. Osaki," replies Chuck, "but why didn't you put all of that to good use, like in politics or something?"

Mr. Osaki pauses briefly. "In my country, the Tea Master is held above politics. He is the great solver of many bureaucratic issues and the strategist for military council. There are only a handful of these noble men left. I fear it will be a lost art form someday. That is why I have chosen you as my subjects, to enlighten your thoughts and open your minds to take control of your lives by consciously acting against the emotions of your heart in the passion of anger but instead use your heads for solutions to your problems."

Steve yawns. "You said you have something to give us for agreeing to stop using your garden as a short cut." With that, Steve's head tilts to the side and he's off to la-la land. In his dream, a much younger version of Mai Ling glides down the staircase to a large, open table, where only he is sitting. The room darkens and the front door cracks open, allowing red light to bleed into the room. Suddenly, a gigantic man with the face of an Alaskan Husky steps into the room.

The man and Mai Ling exchange looks, then in a sudden move, she runs across the floor, grabbing the ancient sword of General Yao, preparing for battle with the half-man, half-beast creature.

He screams out, "I am Xtar, son of Zeowitch, king of the wolves! I am here for him. He will feed us for many days!"

She steps in front of Steve. "No, he's mine."

Steve is relieved for a second, until he sees his reflection in a mirror on the distant wall. He has been transformed and is, in fact, a giant hot dog in between a super large bun!

He tries to get to his feet, but his feet are gone! He flops to the ground, trying to wiggle away from his frenzied predators. *Cling, clang!* The metal blade of Mai Ling's sword clashes against the armor of the giant beast.

"He-yah!" Mai Ling pokes the eyes of Xtar as she quickly scales his body with a running flip.

"Ouch!" Steve screams, waking from his brief dream.

Chuck laughs, as Osaki places the hair he plucked from Steve's head in his hand.

"My gift to you," Mr. Osaki says, "is that I shall teach you how to rid yourselves of your bully once and for all."

They agree. "OK, but how do we do that?"

He walks over to the kitchen counter picking up an old black and white camera that is sitting next to the coffee machine. He turns to Steve, hands him the camera and says, "It all starts with a plan and a good cup of tea." Steve takes the camera, smiling from ear to ear.

Chapter Sixteen

Hip hop Tea

Steve pulls a few pictures from his book bag. "I still can't believe he gave me this camera. It has to be worth a couple of hundred bucks!"

Chuck responds, reaching for the pictures. "Let me see those." He continues, "I can't believe he got pictures of the fight with Junior lying flat on his back!"

They laugh and exchange high-fives and dap. Steve says, "You know what, though? Why didn't he tell me about the pictures when he gave me the camera?"

Chuck stops laughing. "Hmm, that's a good question. He did say that he could only point us in the right direction, and that we had the answers that are right before our eyes."

From a distance, Sammy spots the boys walking to the

parlor. He runs, catching up with them. "What's up, Steve? What's up, Chuck? I missed you guys. Where have you been?" Sammy calls to the boys, who notice that his English is much improved.

Chuck replies. "Taking care of some very important business."

Sammy responds. "Oh. Are you going to get some ice cream?"

Steve turns to Sammy. "No, Sammy. Today is not a fun day, unfortunately. We have some very important business to tend to, but if you want to come along, you can. Just know that this could be potentially disastrous."

Sammy smiles, pulling a stack of CD's from his bag. "Look, I got the new JZ CD and Tupac."

Steve snatches the CD's from his hand. "Let me see those. JZ's retired and Tupac is dead."

Sammy replies, "So? They are a legends in my country."

Chuck adds his two cents. "No, he's right Steve. They're both legends in their own right. Tupac's a great rapper—maybe the best of all time."

Steve can't believe what he's hearing. "OK, so he's a legend, but he's dead! Dead guys can't keep putting out new albums all the time."

Chuck stops in his tracks. "That's it!"

Steve stares him in his face. "What's it?"

Chuck pauses to collect his thoughts. "OK, Mr. Osaki said that we should call and set up the meeting with Junior on our own turf and on our terms. We did that. Then he said that every generation has one thing that is the great mutual force—the one great commonality."

The boys hang onto his every syllable of his words.

Chuck continues. "Music! For our generation the common denominator is music—hip hop, to be more specific."

Steve is pleased with Chuck's discovery, patting him on the back. "You're amazing, you know that?"

Chuck reaches for more of Sammy's CD's. "Sammy, can I see your CD's?"

Sammy nods his head as Chuck continues. "Sammy, I'm going to need to take a few of these for an exchange, but I'll replace them over the weekend with my allowance if you trust me."

Sammy hands over his bag to Chuck. "OK, I trust you."

The boys continue on to the parlor, where they anxiously prepare for the arrival of the older gang of boys, but they have a well-thought-out plan for their unsuspecting adversary. Thirty minutes later, Junior walks in with his bunch of thugs. They pull up seats to the table, where Steve and Chuck sit. Chuck cues Sammy to bring a round of drinks to the table. Sammy politely places the drinks in front of every boy at the table.

Junior's reaction shows that he is surprised by the gesture of kindness shown by the boys.

Just as he is about to speak, Chuck cuts him short, being sure to take the lead in the discussion, as suggested by Mr. Osaki. "Junior, you may be wondering why we have invited you here as our guests. Well, Steve and I have decided it was time that we sit down at the table with you and your boys and have a conversation, like real men."

Junior and his gang laugh. He takes a sip from his cup and spits it on the floor. "Now that's funny! You want to talk to us like men? And what is this, tea?"

Chuck replies, "Yes, it is tea. If I may be so bold as to ask, what is it that you want from us? Is it to put fear into our hearts, to intimidate us, to hurt us, or to bully us around, taking our money and possessions?"

Junior laughs. "You pretty much nailed it. I'd say all of the above."

Steve rises from his chair. "That's not cool man!"

The older boys jump from their chairs itching for a good fight.

Chuck remains calm, waving Steve back into his seat. "Let

me handle this. Look, Junior, what would you say if I told you we aren't scared of you anymore?"

Junior pauses, then looks at his boys. "Then maybe we need to try a little harder." They break into laughter, as Steve hands Chuck a folder from the book bag.

Chuck's demeanor takes on a more serious tone. "OK, I see that we are going to have to go there for you to take us serious." Chuck pulls a contract from the folder, setting it in front of Junior. Junior opens the folder, only to see photos of him lying on the ground, with Chuck standing triumphantly above him.

Junior's mouth drops, doubtful of what he sees. In addition to the photos of his losing fight to a 6th grader, other photos of the gang spray- painting graffiti on the walls of the high school gym are in the bunch.

Junior's temper flares, bringing his face to a flush deep red. "Where did you get these?"

Sammy walks away from the table, while Steve slides his chair back, in anticipation of the power struggle that is about to break out.

Chuck keeps his cool and plays out the tactic of confusion, as used by Mr. Osaki. Chuck momentarily sits quietly, then avoids the direct question asked by Junior. "Junior, your day has come, see, 'cause I realize that you really aren't much different from the rest of us. You're not some inner city street kid, nor are you the thug you want everyone to believe you are. You are one of us who got lost somewhere along the way."

Junior slams his cup to the floor. The owner looks over to the table to make sure Chuck and the kids are not in over their heads. Junior stands over Chuck, threatening him and waving his fist. "You little punk, you're going to give me these pictures or else!"

Chuck responds. "Please, retake your seat. Let's remain civilized about this."

A shocker to Steve, Sammy, and Junior's, gang he actually decides to cooperate, retaking his seat to hear the rest of what

Chuck has to say.

Chuck continues. "As I was saying, what you have before you is an agreement that you will agree to stop bullying us or anyone in our neighborhood. If you choose to ignore the terms of this agreement, copies of the photos you have in your hands will be sent to the police department, the principal of the high school, and oh, yeah, the ones of me beating you up? Let's just say that every kid from here to the state line will get a copy by email."

Junior is speechless, sitting back in his chair, trying to absorb the information he has been hit with. Chuck shows a strong poker face, calmly awaiting Junior's reaction. Knowing that Junior may not be entirely sold on the idea, it is time to enact rule number two of the Tea Ceremony: servitude. Mr. Osaki says that all things work better when both sides win.

Chuck is about to pull the CD's from the bag when Steve grabs him and leans into his ear, whispering, "Do we really have to give away the CD's?"

Chuck, feeling that the tables have turned and he is now on top, pulls away from Steve. "Relax, I've got this."

Chuck pulls a couple of rap CD's from the bag. Among them are JZ, Nelly, Snoop Dogg, and Eminem. Confusion swells in the thugs faces as the CD's scatter across the table.

Chuck allows them to pick up the CD's. "Junior, we would like to offer these CD's as a measure of good faith. You have my word that none of these pictures will reach the hands of the authorities as long as me and my friends are free of harm."

Junior picks up one of the CD's. "You mean you won't rat us out and you're going to give us your CD's, too? But why?"

Chuck looks at Steve, then turns to Junior. "Because it is better to have gained a friend than to fight an enemy."

Junior and his gang rise from their seats and hustle happily toward the door with their new CDs. Junior turns to Chuck with a smile. "Hey, you guys are all right!" Junior walks through the door. Sammy, Steve and Chuck exchange hugs side by side as Chuck replies, "I know."

Chapter Seventeen

Code Red Elixir

It seems as though the days are getting colder by the second, with the outside temperature dropping into the low 40s during the day. The kids are dressing warmer, with their sweaters and bubble coats, trying to fend off the cold weather and even stay warm in their classes.

But then there is Mr. Pettycoat's class—maybe the only class in the entire building with working heat, but the problem is that it works too well.

Sitting beside Ieka and Ms. Elle, Steve pulls a slightly melted chocolate bar from his pocket, offering it to the girls. "Here, you want this?"

Ieka responds, "I don't want that melted thing!"

Ms. Elle waives the bar away from her face. "Me either."

Though it was only a few weeks earlier, the two girls who were neck in neck in the fistfight of the decade have now become close friends through learning about the challenges and culture of each other. Funny how things like that work out.

Chuck walks up to the group, with Sammy by his side. "Hey, boys and girls! You wanna hear something cool?"

They look at Chuck with interest as he continues. "I am working on a potion that influences the hormones in our bodies to persuade a person to develop a fondness for its desired target."

Steve spits out, "You mean a love potion? Chuck, I thought you came up with some silly concoctions before, but this has to be the worst one yet."

The girls are interested in what he has to say. Ms. Elle asks, "That sounds really interesting, but how is it supposed to work?"

He lifts a test tube into the air. "It's really rather simple. The metabolic makeup of the contents within this tube mix with a specific amount of $H2O$ and carbon molecules extracted from the air."

The girls are in awe of Chuck's genius. Steve interrupts. "Yeah, that sounds great in theory, but does it work?"

Ieka comes to the defense of Chuck's potion. "Steve, stop being such a butthead! At least he's doing something with his time. Besides, it beats these boring assignments Mr. Pettycoat gives us."

Chuck sees a bottle of soda sticking out of Ms. Elle's purse. He asks, "Ms. Elle, would you mind if I have that soda? I think it will give my potion just the right element that it is missing."

She answers, "Sure. It's Mountain Dew Code Red. Will that work for you?" Chuck takes the soda, takes a sip, swishing it in his mouth from side to side. "It's perfect; it has the right blend of sugar, sodium and coloration to give the potion the right taste and presentation."

At the Bunsen burner, Steve leans in closely to the flame,

holding the broken frame above it. Chuck runs up behind him, grabbing his wrist and pulling the frame away from the flames.

Steve snaps at him. "What are you doing? Let me go! I'm trying to fix this frame."

Chuck sees the frustration in his face and decides that he must tactfully approach this situation. "Steve, I know how you feel about getting that frame fixed, but you can't mend broken rock with fire, no matter how hot it gets."

A look of disappointment comes over Steve's face. "But how do I fix it? No shop in town will take it."

Chuck says, "That's the million dollar question. How do you fix something you don't have the glue for? I don't know, but I'll find an answer for you."

Sammy lights a paper towel in the flame of the burner. Chuck races to Sammy's aid before Mr. Pettycoat sees the flame. Chuck returns to his workstation, where he carefully blends the Mountain Dew with his current mixture. Adding a couple of drops of ginseng root and a half an Aspirin to the formula so that it will absorb into the bloodstream faster, he completes his formula.

Chuck raises the tube into the air. Peering at it through his specs, he sees it is ready for testing. Chuck glances around the room, trying to find a guinea pig to sample the finished test product.

Steve stomps over to Chuck, frustrated with his situation. "Is that it? Is it done?"

Chuck grins, knowing that if he chooses his words carefully, Steve will likely volunteer to try the potion. The girls walk up at about the same time, with Steve holding the tube in his hand.

Ieka asks, "Steve, what are you doing with that?"

Steve gently swirls the mixture around in the tube. "I'm going to try it."

Ms. Elle blushes at the mere thought of Steve making himself sick. "But you don't even know what it does."

Chuck adds quickly, "Actually, it is designed to make you

105

fall in love with the first person you see. This is just a tester sample, so I expect that its effects won't be long–lasting, but if my calculations are correct, it will work."

Steve lifts the tube into the air, places it against his lips, and the florescent red fluid whizzes down his throat.

Steve stands quietly as the kids carefully observe his behavior. Suddenly his hands start shaking uncontrollably and his eyes roll back in his head! His breaths become short and he grabs for his neck! He starts wobbling from side to side.

"Oh, I feel woozy! Everything is getting dark! Chuck, Ieka, Ms. Elle— where are you?" He throws his hands into the air, as they flail around out of control.

Ieka grabs his left arm, Ms. Elle grabs his right arm, and Chuck steps in front of him, smacking his face and trying to get him back. Steve jumps away from them, nearly falling to the floor he is laughing so hard.

Chuck glares at his watch, punching the timing button on the side. Steve continues to blurt out in laughter, "Ha, ha, ha! I really had you fooled! You thought something was really happening, didn't you? Ha, ha, ha! That's too funny!"

Chuck keeps his stern face. Ignoring Steve, he picks up the sheet that holds the formula of the potion. Chuck's face says more than words ever could, with his eyes squinting together, his forehead wrinkling together, and his lips pouching out, reading over his notes. "Ahh, I see! Just as I expected, three minutes precisely."

Ms. Elle approaches him. "Chuck, don't you care that Steve is mocking you, making you look like a fool?"

Ieka suggests, "Yeah, I can shut him up for you!"

Steve continues laughing as hard as he possibly can without drawing the attention of Mr. Pettycoat. All of a sudden he grips his stomach. "Chuck, my stomach's hurting. What's going on?"

Chuck smiles, gloating from within. "I'll tell you what's happening. The cells of the lining of your digestive tract are undergoing a temporary destabilization, thereby releasing its contents—better known as an I.B.M., or intense bowel movement."

Ieka says under her breath, having been enlightened by Chuck, "I thought I.B.M. was a computer company."

Steve grabs his butt. "What? Oh, this ain't funny! I gotta go! I gotta go! I've got to go to the bathroom!"

The girls giggle all over themselves at Chuck showing off his advanced knowledge of chemistry.

Steve continues. "I think this is gonna be a big one, Chuck! Maybe a three flusher!"

Ieka points, "There's a bathroom across the hall."

Steve runs frantically through the door into the bathroom without thinking in search of immediate relief.

The girls laugh even harder. Ms. Elle adds, "Ieka you're wrong for that. You know that's the girls' bathroom!"

She replies, "I know, but won't it be funny if somebody finds him in the girls' bathroom? Anyway, he's always pulling pranks on us. Why not get him back for a change?"

Chuck adds, "He might be in for a little trouble if someone does walk in."

Ms. Elle and Ieka catch their breath. Ms. Elle asks, "Why is that?"

"Only because the potion is designed so that whoever his eyes land upon first after his bowels are clean will be the person he temporarily falls in love with."

Ieka says, "Guess it's a good thing we sent him to the girls' bathroom."

They all laugh, but Mr. Pettycoat's attention shifts to their side of the room and he moves toward their area to see what is so funny. He steps up to the kids. "Chuck, is there something going on here?"

Chuck keeps his eyes locked on his burner. "No, sir, just trying to get the project done."

Satisfied with his answer, Mr. Pettycoat walks back to his desk, but he drops his wallet on the way. Ms. Elle, relieved from the stress, asks, "So, Chuck, since it looks like your potion works, what are you going to call it?"

The wallet lies on the floor, unattended and unnoticed. The kids continue talking about poor Steve, who is stuck on the toilet. "Code Red Elixir," exclaims Chuck as his foot slips on the wallet.

Chapter Eighteen

Brutha from Anutha Mutha

Steve says to himself, "I don't get it. It was hurting so bad just a minute ago." *Blurp! Rumble! Rumble!* goes his stomach. "Ooh, I need help," Steve says, as his stomach continues to bubble within.

With nearly ten minutes gone by, Steve has an idea that just might work. He decides to tickle his stomach to see if he can get some relief when suddenly—*Warp!*— with one big long fart, it all comes loose at once!

"Yes!" echoes through the bathroom into the hallway, where Principal Winkleshire hears the loud shout in the distance. She abruptly turns, heading to the girls' bathroom.

Inside the classroom, Chuck and the girls eagerly await the sound of the flush from the bathroom. *Whoosh!*

The girls giggle. Chuck says, "That's one."

Whoosh! Chuck adds, "That's two!"

Sammy walks up to the group. "Hey, where's Steve?"

They laugh. Chuck lets him in on the prank. "He's in the bathroom."

Sammy realizes that there is something more to Steve being in the bathroom than he is being told. "Is he ok?"

Ieka tries to keep from cracking a smile. "I'm sure he'll be just fine once that red stuff gets through his system."

The kids continue dancing in laughter, when it comes to Ieka that Chuck wasn't making the potion for Steve, so exactly who was he making it for? Ieka grabs Chuck by the arm. "Chuck, who are you making this stuff for anyway?"

Chuck squirms away from her grasp, but he can't hide the guilt on his face. "Uh, nobody in particular."

Ms. Elle realizes that it is probably Ieka's sister. "Aw, I'll bet it's for your sister. You know he has a crush on her."

Chuck jumps away from Ieka, expecting to feel the sting of her punch.

Like a bolt of lightening, Ieka grabs Chuck by the ear. With a hard twist she says, "Listen to me, boy! If you give that stuff to my sister, I swear. . ."

Chuck interrupts, digging himself clear of her wrath. "Relax! Obviously it doesn't have the desired effects to give it to someone like your sister. I wouldn't be that stupid."

Ieka calms back down, sitting atop the desk between Chuck and Ms. Elle.

As Chuck re-preps the burner, he whispers under his breath, "Not until I get it right; then watch me win her over."

Suddenly—*Whoosh!*— the third flush comes from the bathroom. Chuck and the girls nearly lose it. "That's the third flush. It's a three flusher!" Chuck takes a bow, as if he has just won the state championship wrestling match.

Water builds rapidly in the toilet bowl, swirling brown toilet paper to the lid of the bowl with the water continuing to run.

With a mini-candy bar hanging from his mouth, Steve feverishly jiggles the handle, trying to get the water to stop running. The water spews over onto the floor, wetting the bottom of Steve's jeans. Rushing to unlock the door, Steve climbs from the narrow stall, dropping the candy bar onto the flooding bathroom floor. At this moment, Steve must make a decision as to whether to leave and let the water continue flooding the bathroom or take responsibility and get some help to prevent damage to the floor.

Opting for what is only the right thing to do, Steve makes a mad dash down the hallway, running right smack into Principal Winkleshire. Nearly out of breath, he explains, "Ms. Winkleshire, I'm so glad I ran into you. There's a problem in the bathroom! The water's running all over the floor! We have to hurry! This way!"

They hurry down the hallway, as she follows him to the bathroom, where water is already coming from under the door. She takes the 2-way radio from her belt, only to realize that the batteries are dead. Turning to Steve, she says calmly, "This is going to be a mess."

Steve glances into the classroom, where the commotion has everyone in the class watching Steve and the principal outside.

"Come with me this way, young man," says the principal, walking at a fast pace to an unknown destination. Steve follows her, feeling empty and hollow like a sheep being led to slaughter, but something inside stirs up an attraction for the principal. His heart begins to beat uncontrollably, his pupils dilate, and his palms become clammy. Is he catching the flu, or is there something more that ails him? For the life of him, Steve can't figure out what is going on with him.

For a moment, Steve sees the principal in a different light. After all, she is a very attractive lady. She is very young for such a position, and she is responsive every time he has needed to speak to her. She is his equal—and his momentary love interest. In an attempt to impress the principal, Steve starts

111

dishing compliments her way. "Ms. Winkleshire, did I ever tell you how pretty your eyes are? And that shade of your lipstick compliments your eyes so well. And you're always dressed so nicely. And, I um, I love the way you always put your hair in that style."

Nothing seems to be working, for she ignores him, remaining focused on her intended plan.

Coming to his senses, Steve realizes that with every step they grow closer and closer to her office, where he is sure he will receive suspension or detention at best. What was he thinking, giving the principal compliments? His mind begins to wonder how he will explain this series of unfortunate events to his mother. To his surprise, it becomes clear that they aren't headed for her office at all; instead, it's worse—much worse. They are heading for the Creepy Closet, a.k.a. the janitor's closet!

Slowly and cautiously, she pokes her head through the crack in the door of the closet, into the dim dwelling where the monster stays. Does she know? Could it be that the flesh of the poor old janitor was eaten by the beast Chuck caught a glimpse of? Maybe she was so angry with him that she has decided to teach him a serious lesson by leaving him alone, locked in the room, awaiting his fate with the unknown "thing."

"Harold? Harold are you in there?" she calls into the room, opening the door a little further.

Steve is taken aback, asking, "Harold?"

She smiles. "Yes, Harold, he's my younger brother," she says, walking further into the room. Harold sits calmly on a couple of stacked milk crates, playing his favorite X Box game: Mortal Combat V. The graphics quality isn't very good on his black and white television, and he can't hear them with his earphones on.

Steve's eyes scan the big fellow in front of them. He notices that his kinky hair is similar to that of his own wooly naps, and his skin tone is noticeably darker than Ms. Winkie's pale white skin.

Steve can't hold back his question any longer. "Ms. Winkleshire, he's your brother, but how is that? He's so big and brown, and you're so. . .?"

Placing her words delicately, "Small? That's a reasonable question to ask. Well your answer is that we share the same father, but come from different mothers."

Steve accepts her answer. "So that would make him your 'brutha from anutha mutha?'" She grins. "I guess that would be true in the truest sense."

Before making a move, she pauses. "Good observation."

Steve's reluctance to move forward into the room is obvious. She rests her hand on Steve's shoulder. "Don't be afraid Steve, I know he's a big guy and a little frightful, but he's not much older than you, mentally."

Steve looks up at her. "You mean he's. . ."

She cuts him off. "Handicapped."

Steve sighs. "Like me."

She crouches down to see eye-to-eye with Steve. "I am aware of your condition, Steve, and yes it is a handicap. But like Harold, you too must learn to overcome the obstacles life deals you. You know, Steve, part of the reason I took this job was to show children like you that an entire world of opportunities exists for people just like you. You don't have to accept what people think is your place in society; instead, you can create it if you just know what you want."

A tear draws up in his eye. Trying to wipe it away, it rolls gently down his fingertip. There, in the dusty confines of the janitor's closet, Steve sees that no matter what people say about Ms. Winkie, she has a heart of gold.

She continues. "That means that there's more to life than fast cars, fast girls, and fast cash like you see on television, young man. Sure, you can be an entertainer, a ball player, or even a rapper, if you want. But have you ever considered a career in horticulture, podiatry or optometry?

Steve is blown away by the vast amount of information he is gaining in just a few words of conversation with this woman. He replies, "No, I don't even know what those things are."

She responds, "Look them up. In fact, do your research, because if you have to spend your life working to make money, it should be something that you enjoy. Understood?"

He nods his head.

From out of nowhere, the voice of Confucius echoes in his head, saying almost the same thing the principal is saying. Seeing that she has his undivided attention, Ms. Winkie stands to resume her power. "Just know that I am proud of you, Steve. I know it hasn't been easy, coming here as a new student, but you have adjusted very well with your new friends who understand you *and* your condition." She closes in on Harold as he removes the headphones from his head and the advice churns in Steve's mind.

"Steve, this is my younger brother Harold. Harold, this is one of my new students, Steve," she says, introducing the two.

They exchange handshakes, but Steve is compelled to speak up. "Harold. I'm very sorry. My friend and I were sent here by our teacher, but we ran out before we had a chance to talk with you 'cause we thought you where a monster."

He is silent for a moment, then looks at his sister with a blank stare, then smiles. "It's OK. I thought you were fat, but you're just big!"

They share laughs, relieving the tension that could have caused problems.

The running water from the toilet continues to flow from under the bathroom door, while Harold, Steve and the principal have their moment. The water finds its way into the classroom, carrying with it a piece of freshly used toilet paper and a little brown mini-candy bar that the class thinks is a part of a turd. The kids move into a tight semi-circle in the back of the room. The water inches into the room, pushing the turd across the floor, making the girls scream.

Through the halls, bouncing off the cork ceilings, the screams are carried into the janitor's closet. The principal remembers the reason she came there. "Harold grab a mop and bucket; we've got work for you."

They head off to the bathroom. As they walk down the hallway, Steve feels a sense of accomplishment for not only for doing the right thing, but for owning up to his responsibility. The best part of it all is that Ms. Winkie has no idea that it was Steve who clogged up the toilet in the girls' bathroom, of all places. Or does she?

Heading back into Mr. Pettycoat's interrupted class, Steve takes the chance to thank Ms. Winkie for her advice. She smiles, pulling a piece of dangling toilet paper from his tucked-in shirt, and winks at him as she walks off.

Steve pats Harold on the back. "Thanks for the help, man. Friends?"

Harold slaps him a high-five. "Sure, we're friends. Maybe you can play my X Box with me sometime."

Steve nods his head, then strolls into class, where he's been gone for almost 20 minutes; he is certain to be the center of attention.

Chapter Nineteen

All Broken Things Can Mend

She holds the phone away from her ear. "Someone wants to talk with you."

Steve can't think of anyone who would call at this time of the night, so he asks who it is. She smiles, showing her pearly whites and handing him the phone. "Just answer it and find out for yourself."

Steve takes the phone, unsure of how to feel about the game his mom is playing.

"Hello?" he says with the confidence shaking in his voice.

"Hey, son," he hears from the other end of the phone. It is the voice he has been dying to hear.

"Dad! Hey, Dad, where have you been? I've missed you!"

He responds, "I've missed you too! I've been away for some

time. I was in Iraq for the war, now I'm on a covert mission: special ops. Can't talk long—just wanted to let you and your mom know how much I miss you guys."

With his eyes swelling up with tears, Steve's emotions overwhelm him and he breaks down, sobbing. He drops the phone into middle of the bed, and his mom grabs him, hugging and squeezing him while kissing his forehead. She picks up the phone and hands it back to him.

Steve says to his dad, "I'm sorry, Dad. I can't talk right now. When can I see you?"

In a loving voice he replies, "Soon, little man, soon."

Steve kisses his mom on the cheek and walks out of the room as she finishes her conversation with his dad. As their conversation winds up, Steve walks back into the room.

"Did you know?"

She looks at him with an unusual expression. "Did I know what? That he was in Iraq?" She ponders the question for a moment. "No, they called him up shortly after we decided to take a break. I was just as much in the dark as you were. I hadn't heard from him and had no idea where he was, so when you asked, I didn't know what to tell you, Steve."

Steve probes, "But why, Mom? Why would you leave Dad in the first place?"

She pulls him close. "I wish I knew the answer to that one. There are some things we do as adults that even we don't understand. What's important is that you know I love you dearly, and your father loves you too. Together or apart, you will always have our hearts."

He positions himself under his mom's arm comfortably while thinking about what she is saying. "Will you guys ever get back together?"

Stroking his fuzzy fro, she smiles. "Can't say for sure, but after tonight, I think so."

Steve sighs with relief, realizing that there is a greater hope that his parents may still get back together.

What a day for Steve—with the potion, the principal, the fixed picture frame, and now this! There just doesn't seem to be a way to top this day any better than to go to sleep, knowing that his dad has been away serving his country, has returned in once piece, and that he'll be seeing him soon.

Steve picks up the frame, noticing how carefully it was mended back together so you can hardly tell that it was ever broken.

On the back of the frame is attached a note which reads, "I got a little help from our new friend who has a shop class; his name is Junior. Hope this cheers you up a little. Sorry about the prank on you earlier. Hope we're still cool, Chuck." Steve pulls the note from the frame and studies it for a moment. Attached to the bottom of the note is a small device that looks like a little metal pill. The note continues. "By the way, this was found in the frame. It's a GPS remote satellite transmitter giving your location anywhere in the world. Hold on to it; it might be good for something."

Was Chuck really on to something? Sure the prank on him earlier was mean and juvenile, but it wasn't anything he wouldn't have done himself if he had thought of it first. But the gesture of fixing the frame and enlisting the help of their once archenemy was beyond his comprehension, unless the transmitter was also part of a prank. Even if it were a joke, the most important thing was that the frame was fixed.

Right then Steve realizes that in Chuck he has a friend for life. Only a few weeks before, he was a new kid on the block with no friends and recently separated parents. But now he has found a best friend in Chuck and good friends in Sammy, Ieka and Ms. Elle—friendships that he wouldn't trade for all the money in the world. Steve relaxes his head on his pillow, knowing that he still has the love and support of his mom and his dad.

With the rest of the school year ahead, he knows more challenges await him, but the most important key to his

119

happiness—love between family and friends—doesn't have to change; it can adjust. One thing stays on his mind, however. What if Chuck is right? What is the probability that he and his friends' fathers, all involved in the military, have recently relocated to the same area? How could he end up with an ex-Marine teacher who just relocated, too? His dad is special ops? And the planted GPS transmitter. . .

This is all too much for Steve to take in. His mind needs rest. If they are all in on some big secret mission, he'll just have to wait to save the world until another day. And with that, he drifts off to sleep, tightly clinching to the stone that has been reunited in both the frame and his separated parents, whom he is sure will get back together.

About the Author

Deronte' L. Smith is an award winning writer and director of motion picture film who realized his dream of writing a piece for pre-teenage children with the completion of the first book in a series entitled The Fantastical Adventures of Sleepy Steve. Founded on the principles of Twain, Elliot and other literary greats before him, Smith sought to simply tell the story. His imagination spans

Deronte' Smith

across a time continuum dating back 500 years before Christ to modern day issues that our children face daily.

Smith, who currently resides in Georgia, is a Kentucky native where his roots connect him to likes of Mohammad Ali, George Clooney and Ashley Judd – all having stellar careers and grown up just down the road from his hometown. Graduating with a bachelor's in English from the University of Kentucky in 1996, Smith landed a position with a local car dealership giving him his first job out of college.

In the subsequent years, Smith, an avid writer, put down his pen and focused on earning money and climbing the corporate ladder which lead him to an eventual move. "I love Kentucky but Atlanta has been very good to me. I often tell myself I have two homes," Smith says of the move he made to Atlanta Georgia in 1998. Putting the advice of his family to the side, Smith moved with the confidence that everything would work out fine. And in due time, he was sure he would pursue his gift of writing professionally.

It was not until the fall of 1999 that Smith's life would be forever changed by the untimely death of his beloved mother.

121

"She was my mother, my support system and my best friend. Her beauty and strength was one of a kind, she cannot be replaced," Smith says reflecting of his loss. This came at a time when he was negotiating the purchase of a new home, establishing a new relationship while closing out an old one and at the top of his game in the sales force when the devastating news arrived one afternoon that his mother had passed in her sleep. "It was the most difficult thing I have ever had to deal with but in retrospect it empowered me in a way that I never expected. I had to be all grown up for my family which then allowed me to tap into those emotions swirling about wildly in my heart and mind."

In the spring of 2002, the idea was born that one boy dealing with real life issues could find a renewed sense of pride in his family while gaining life experiences dealing with the personal relationships of his friends – and Sleepy Steve was born. Shaping and molding Steve into a believable character was a task well within Smith's grasp having worked as an after school counselor with the YMCA while in college. Additionally, having study behavioral and child psychology gave Smith greater insight into the behavioral patterns children often display. "If there is one thing I hope that people take away from this book, it is that we as artists, entertainers, parents and educators must assume responsibility for the lack luster performance our children are showing in school."

Reuniting the Stone is the first of the five book Sleepy Steve series guaranteed to bring a smile to the face of any age reader. Smith is currently nearing the completion of book two with fans already wanting more. There is sure to be a ground swell of fans and critics alike when Sleepy Steve makes his mark.